SERIES

SILVER

SERIES

Louise Cooper writes:
Ask visitors to Cornwall what they love about it, and the chances are they'll talk about the golden beaches, the dramatic cliffs and the sense of ancient magic that the land evokes. I agree – but in the years since I've lived here I've also become fascinated by another side of Cornwall: the river creeks with their lushly wooded valleys, that seem a world away from the thundering Atlantic surf.

The creeks have a more secret magic; the kind that, at certain moments, gives rise to a tingling feeling at the nape of my neck, and a half-eager, half-fearful desire to look quickly over my shoulder, expecting to glimpse . . . *something* . . . which reason says can't really be there. It's as if another, unseen dimension is quietly shadowing our everyday world.

I've felt the presence of that unseen world many times, though – so far – I haven't met it face to face. But sometimes, I believe, the barriers come down and the two worlds meet. And that is what inspired this story.

DEMON CROSSING
LOUISE COOPER

**Hodder
Children's
Books**

A division of Hodder Headline Limited

1

In Tom McCarthy's opinion, his parents couldn't have picked a more appropriate date to move house. April Fools' Day – it summed it up perfectly. When Mum woke him at five o'clock this morning he had wondered for a moment if the whole thing really *was* an April Fools joke, and she and Dad would suddenly turn round and laugh at him for falling for the wind-up. But the fact that he was in a sleeping bag, the house was completely empty except for a few kitchen bits, and the SOLD board was right outside his bedroom window, told their own story. At seven-thirty he had struggled blearily into the car, and they had set off on the trail of yesterday's furniture van. Now, six hours and three stops later, they were in the depths of Cornwall, it was belting down with rain (April *showers*?), and Tom was definitely starting to feel very unreal indeed.

He still hadn't really grasped the fact that they were moving. It had all happened so quickly, and from the beginning he had swung wildly between feelings of excitement and panic. For as long as he could remember, Mum and Dad had had half-baked ideas about living in some kind of countrified bliss; but Tom had never thought they were serious. Wrong. When Dad was made redundant, it gave them the chance they had been waiting for. Trevenna Mill came up for sale in the same week that Dad had got his redundancy money, and it was as if the gods had conspired to make everything fall into place.

Even for a city boy like Tom, the prospect of moving to an old water mill near the south Cornish coast had quite a lot going for it. Cornwall was a different world. There'd be boats, surfing, fishing – loads of things that just weren't possible in a city. Not a bad life in all.

Mum and Dad hadn't taken him with them when they drove down to see the mill. However, when they returned with the news that they were definitely buying it, it began to sound as if the new world was going to be different in ways that Tom hadn't considered. The mill was in a valley, Dad said, which ran down to a creek, which in turn led to a river and then to the sea. So far, so good. But when Tom started to ask more detailed questions, his parents had suddenly become very cagey. The mill, they told him, was probably seventeenth century or thereabouts, with a separate house and a garden, at the top of a wooded valley. They used the word *old* a great deal, and the fact that they had 'forgotten' to take any photos on their visit alerted Tom's suspicions. What weren't they telling him? The excitement and the panic had started tugging him in different directions, and now he didn't know what he felt.

Well, he was about to find out. The narrow road, which was bordered by high, overgrown stone walls, called 'hedges' and fields on either side, bent suddenly, and the car lurched as the bend turned out to be a lot sharper than Dad had expected. He said, 'Oops,' and got the car under control again. A little further on the road forked, and a signpost declaring TREVENNA 1 pointed to the left fork.

'This is us.' Dad turned the wheel (very cautiously this time) and they swung into an even narrower lane which progressed in a series of zigzags. The trees crowded in until the grey sky almost vanished completely, and Dad added, 'Almost there! Everyone OK?'

Tom tried to think of a wisecrack answer to that, but words failed him. OK? Well, he supposed he was. Provided he ignored the fact that he was moving to a house he had never seen, in a place he had never been to, away from all the friends and activities and familiar haunts that he had built up during his whole life . . . Aware that panic was getting the upper hand again, he tried to think about the compensations. Fresh air. (All right, if you liked that sort of thing.) Space. (Yes, that could be good. Couldn't it . . . ?) New things to do, new places to explore. (And no cinemas, no shops, no entertainments, no buses to get to them even if they had existed . . .)

Something hit him on the head, and a small pink toy gorilla fell into his lap. He started, and screwed round in time to see his sister, Katy, who was nearly two, crowing with delight in her toddler-seat.

'Sorry, Tom,' said Mum, who was sitting beside Katy. 'She's getting quick.'

Tom pulled a hideous face at his sister and dropped the toy gorilla into Mum's outstretched hand. Katy grinned. She'd been asleep for most of the journey, but was now wide awake and lively. She was too young to care what was waiting at the other end. All she knew was that they were in the Brrm-Brrm, and that usually meant going somewhere where there'd be Skweemies and Blurgers for Kitten-Kat. Katy's life revolved round ice-creams and burgers, and Tom wondered how she would react when she finally worked out that they were living about five thousand light-years from the nearest McDonald's.

The road turned again then, and there was Trevenna village. Tom couldn't see much through the pelting rain, but he had an impression of some white-painted bungalows, then a tight row of much older stone houses, one of which had a Post Office sign outside. After this came a pub, set back from the road, and then a church with a little graveyard. An even narrower lane led away left by the church, almost doubling back on itself. Dad turned the car into it, and in a short time they were out of the village and going cautiously between more stone hedges, this time with a dense belt of trees to their right. Katy squealed, 'Moo-cow!' though the hedges were much too high for her to see over. Across a tiny stone bridge, with a weed-choked stream running beneath it, then another sign showed to the right, half hidden in the hedge's tangle. It read: TREVENNA MILL ONLY, with an addition underneath: UNSUITABLE FOR HEAVY GOODS VEHICLES. Tom spluttered at the thought of an artic trying to squeeze into the space, opened his mouth to say something about the furniture van, then thought better of it and kept quiet. Another few hundred metres, bumping now on an unmade and rutted surface . . . and, so suddenly that it was almost shocking, the trees opened out and Trevenna Mill rose ahead of them.

Tom stared, transfixed, as all the images he had imagined collapsed in the space of a single moment. The mill was *huge*; a great, tall barn of a building standing in a patch of open land between the lane and the steep, densely wooded valley. Dark stone walls; doorways with no doors; glassless windows gaping open to the weather – the whole place had a lost, dank, decaying look about it, like something out of a horror movie. It also looked as if it would cost a fortune to make it habitable.

Dad glanced sideways, saw the expression on Tom's face, and laughed. 'Don't panic, we're not going to live in that part! That's the actual mill – the house is separate, round the other side.'

'And that *has* got a roof and four walls,' Mum added. 'But isn't it gorgeous?'

Tom didn't even attempt to answer. He was still staring, still mesmerized. Never in all his life had he seen

5

anywhere so unlikely, so . . . so . . . he struggled for an ideal word and came up with *bizarre*. That was it: *bizarre*. It fascinated him. And yet . . .

His thoughts snapped off as the car halted and Dad cut the engine. An extraordinary silence descended, broken only by the swish and patter of rain. A part of Tom was urging him to scramble out of the car and ignore everything else until he had explored the mill from top to bottom. And another part wanted to turn right around and go back the way they had come. Even Katy was silent, staring with round eyes and a bewildered expression.

'Come on,' said Dad. 'It's a bit boggy on this side, so we'd better not try to drive down to the house in case we get stuck. There's a trackway, see it? We'll park here and make a dash. Let's get the house open, then we can come back for the bags.'

There was a kerfuffle when Katy, unstrapped and put into her waterproof, flatly refused to be carried but insisted on walking. Eventually Mum and Dad hurried on ahead, leaving Tom to coax his sister after them. Following at a painfully slow toddler's pace, Tom had plenty of time to get wet – and to look at his new home in more detail. The patch that they were skirting was large, with small reeds growing at its edge. It was certainly boggy; downright waterlogged, in fact, and he wondered what it could possibly have once been. An ornamental lake? Or just a quirk of the land? Whatever the case, just beyond its edge the ground dropped away down a steep bank, and the mill building was at the foot of the bank, on a kind of plateau between it and the sharp drop into the tree-hung valley. As he led Katy down the bank he could see the enormous wooden millwheel, sunk in shadow and green with weed and decay, hanging over a deep, stone-lined channel where the water used to run. A rickety footbridge spanned the channel, coming out from stone supports built into the bank and crossing above and behind the wheel. With a broken rail and many planks missing, it looked lethal. He wondered if the wheel could still turn, and how long it had been since it was last worked.

Katy had stopped to examine a clump of white flowers that grew in the scrubby grass. Tom's hair was dripping already and his shoulders were damp; he tugged on the little girl's hand. 'Come *on*, Kitten-Kat! I'm getting soaked!'

She looked up at him, then at the mill, then at him again, and her face became solemn. Then she stated flatly,

'Monter.'

It was her way of saying 'monster', and Tom was surprised. Monsters were a big bugaboo with Katy, since she had sneaked into his room while he was watching a horror video and scared herself half out of her wits. 'Don't be silly,' he told her, kindly. 'There aren't any monsters here.'

She didn't answer him, but jammed one thumb into her mouth and stared at the mill again.

And for no reason whatsoever, Tom felt a chilly shiver, that had nothing to do with the rain, trickling slowly down his spine.

A week later, the McCarthys were starting to settle in their new home. To Tom's vast relief the house was very different to the mill. It sat squarely in a garden full of weeds, it had no carpets and no central heating, the kitchen was prehistoric, and every time you turned a tap on the plumbing rumbled and clonked and burped as if some metallic gremlin was dying slowly and nastily inside the walls. But the electricity worked, the roof didn't leak, and the rooms were plentiful and big. There was a spare downstairs room where Mum could keep her piano out of Katy's destructive reach, and where she fantasized about maybe starting to teach music again, as she used to do, once Katy was old enough to go to school.

Tom's bedroom looked down the slope of the creek valley. It was twice the size of his old room at home (he wasn't yet able to think of Trevenna as 'home') and once he'd changed a few things, including the gloomy pea-green walls, it would be a pretty good place to hang out and relax. If he leaned out of the window he could see the looming bulk of the mill, and when the weather was fine – though, so far, they hadn't had one completely dry day – he could just glimpse the distant shine of sun on water through the trees.

He had walked down to the creek a couple of times,

on an overgrown but negotiable path from the edge of the garden. There wasn't much to see there: just more trees, the water itself and, when the tide was low enough, a narrow foreshore of sand, shingle and weed, with a disused stone jetty jutting out into the flow. The rain put him off exploring too far. There would be time for that later.

He had been helping to get the house straight, and he had also spent some time exploring the mill with Dad. The boggy patch, he soon learned, was the site of the original millpond. It had been fed by a stream, and when the mill was working a series of sluice gates would let the water through, down the bank and into the stone channel to turn the millwheel. The sluice gates weren't there any more and the stream no longer ran into the pond, but in anything but drought conditions the place was still a mudbath, as Katy discovered to her delight, until Mum sternly banned her from going anywhere near it.

Dad wanted to restore the mill to working order. Tom thought he was crazy; it would take an army of people, and as for the cost . . . the odd bits of part-time van driving and other casual work that Dad was going to do wouldn't go a thousandth of the way towards it. Unless they won the Lottery the idea seemed impossible. But he kept his thoughts to himself. If Dad wanted to have a go, why not? It would be interesting, to say the least.

However, Tom didn't spend as much time as he might

have done helping with the house or exploring the mill – because, two days after they moved in, Mum came home with Dublin.

Dublin blundered into the McCarthys' lives like an eager, slobbering whirlwind. He was an Irish wolfhound, four months old, with long legs, a woolly grey coat and a ridiculous raspberry-coloured tongue. Keeping a dog had never been an option in the city, and Mum had always wanted one. Yes, all right, she *could* have taken more time, and found a sensible-sized puppy, but . . . well, Dublin had just *looked* at her, and that was that.

If Dublin had one aim in life it was to love everyone and be loved by them in return. In the space of two days he had wriggled and licked and barked his way into the affections of them all. Katy adored him, pulling his tail and his ears and climbing all over him. Dublin didn't mind in the least, and would roll on his back, raspberry tongue lolling happily while she did her worst. He latched on to Tom with a kind of fixed adoration and was soon following at his heels wherever he went, gazing at him with a kind of 'You Are My Friend, And Where You Go, I Go Too' determination. Tom's resistance to the puppy's charms lasted about fifteen seconds, and before the McCarthys knew it, Dublin was one of the family.

There were small setbacks. To start with Dublin wasn't house-trained, and mopping up smelly puddles in the kitchen, the hall, the sitting-room and even once on his own duvet was far from Tom's idea of fun. Then there were his new trainers. Dublin prised them out from under Tom's bed, killed them thoroughly and carried the sorry remains downstairs to lay them triumphantly at Tom's feet. He only managed to chew one computer disc, but in the space of a week Mum's hairbrush, Dad's best Levis, two kitchen mats and one of Katy's floppy rag dolls all went the same way as the trainers – which at least proved, Tom thought, that Dublin liked to share his favours equally. It was impossible to yell at him, though, because the daft dog only thought yelling was some new game and responded by writhing all over the floor and barking himself nearly sick with excitement. Every time he barked, Tom started laughing, because it wasn't a proper bark at all but a kind of half-strangled *yowlp* which, considering that Dublin was already nearly the size of an Alsatian and growing fast, made him more ludicrous than ever. Then when he finally got the message that he was in disgrace, he grovelled so hard for forgiveness that it was impossible to stay angry with him.

As well as not being house-trained, Dublin wasn't lead-trained, either, and Tom soon became used to being towed along like a water-skier behind a speedboat as the puppy explored everything.

Then the peculiar thing happened.

Dublin was on his lead, with Tom tearing behind him as usual. They had completed three high-speed circuits of the garden, when the puppy headed eagerly round the side of the house to the mill building. Dad was somewhere in the mill, creating havoc with a crowbar and mallet, and as Tom and the puppy approached the dried-up water channel (which, Tom now knew, was technically called the millrace), Dublin suddenly stopped dead and refused to go another step.

'Come on, you daft dog!' Tom tugged on the lead. 'Walk!'

The word 'walk' didn't have its usual effect. Dublin would not move, but instead lowered his head and began to growl. He was staring fixedly at the water wheel, as if he had seen something that he did *not* like. Tom peered, screwing up his eyes.

'Come on, Dublin! There isn't anything there!'

Dublin growled again. His tail was between his legs now. Then he uttered his peculiar half-yelp, half-bark . . . and for no reason at all, Tom had a flashback to the day they had moved in; him holding Katy's hand, and Katy staring at the mill and saying, 'Monter'.

Dad's head appeared through a gaping window hole. 'What's the matter with him?'

'I don't know,' Tom called back. 'He doesn't like the wheel for some reason.'

'Idiot animal.' Dad waggled a hand to attract Dublin's attention. 'Go on, Dublin! Go with Tom! Walkies, boy!'

Dublin looked at him, and his tail and ears lifted uncertainly. Then he started to back away, pulling hard on the lead.

'He's just being silly,' Dad said. 'Take him off somewhere else. He'll get over it.'

Dublin pulled even harder, and Tom let him have his head. Like Dad, he assumed that the strange behaviour was a one-off, and Dublin was just being awkward. But when it happened again, and then a third time, he suspected there was more to it. Dublin flatly refused to go near the water wheel, and if he was made to go, then he growled and barked and bristled, and would only calm down when he was well away from it again. For the life of him Tom couldn't see anything that could possibly upset the dog. But then animals were said to have a sixth sense, weren't they? And there had been his little sister's strange comment . . .

When the 'walk' with Dublin was finished, he went back into the house. Dublin flopped on to the nearest rug and Tom squatted down beside his sister, who was in her play-pen to keep her out of Mum's way.

'Hi, Kitten-Kat.' He picked up a woolly sheep on wheels that she had tipped over the pen's side. 'Want to come with Tom-Tom and see the big mill?'

Katy looked at him, thought for a few moments, then shook her head vigorously. 'Doh,' she said.

That meant no. 'Why not?' Tom persisted. 'It's a nice mill.'

Another think. Then: 'Isn't!' Katy's face screwed up into a pout. 'Monter!'

So she remembered, and she still thought the same.

13

Interesting . . . 'There's no monster there,' said Tom.

'Is,' Katy argued. '*Nasty* monter!'

Tom knew he had to tread carefully; if he pushed her too far she would start howling, and that would bring Mum, and he'd be in trouble. But he needed to know, so he asked cautiously, 'What sort of monster is it?'

She didn't answer at first, and he thought she was going to clam up. But eventually she blinked and said, 'Sklington.'

'A skeleton?' *Ah*, Tom thought. That was what she had glimpsed on the horror movie: probably she thought all monsters were skeletons. OK – one more question.

'Did you *see* it, Kitten-Kat?'

Her head came up and she gazed at him with big, round eyes. Then, slowly and solemnly, she nodded. 'Nasty sklington,' she said. 'Dubly see it, too.'

Tom stood up. He wasn't going to risk asking her anything more . . . but this was getting a little bit strange. Katy had started to play with her toys again, and Dublin had gone to sleep on the rug. Maybe, he thought, he would just go out to the mill again and take a closer look.

Outside, the sky had taken on a threatening sulphur tinge, and the air was very still, as if it was building up for a storm. Tom could hear the dull thump of Dad's mallet from inside the mill building; he walked towards the race and stopped near the silent water wheel. What *had* frightened Katy and Dublin? All right, the place looked gloomy and menacing – pretty creepy, in fact – which was enough to scare a little kid. But dogs surely didn't have an imagination in the same way as humans.

He looked at the wooden footbridge over the millrace. It was unsafe to actually walk on; but if he at least climbed up to it he would be about level with the top of the wheel, and could get a better overall view. The bank was slippery but negotiable; he went up it, sliding a few times, until he reached the point where the stone piles supported the bridge's end. Then cautiously, testing the strength, he slid one foot on to the first plank of the bridge and leaned forward.

A grumble of thunder sounded in the distance, but it was a long way off and there wasn't any lightning. Tom peered across the dank space of the millrace channel. There was a walkway on the other side, a narrow stone ledge that no one in their right mind would want to negotiate, and the wall was stained with greenish-black streaks. But that was all. It was a decaying old building, nothing more.

'Tom!' An angry shout startled him, and he turned round to see Dad looking out through the window.

'What are you doing up there? I've told you not to go near that bridge, it's dangerous! Get down this instant!'

'Sorry, Dad.' Tom began to slither backwards down the bank. 'I only wanted to—'

'Never mind what you wanted, you *don't* go near it! Understand? If you fell, you'd break your neck!'

Tom said, 'Sorry,' a second time and reached the bottom of the bank. Dad vanished back inside, but Tom knew he would still be watching. He couldn't try again. Puzzled and disappointed, he turned to go back to the house.

On the far side of the millrace, something moved.

Tom jumped and his head jerked back towards the channel and the old wheel. For a moment he thought he must have imagined the movement . . . but then a shape stirred in the gloom on the ledge. His heart started to pound as hard as Dad's hammer as his brain took in the impression of a hunched, crone-like figure crouching in the deep shadow by the wheel. He couldn't see its face – if it had one – for it was shrouded in a hooded cape or cloak of some kind. But a sense of something dark, threatening, *evil*, skimmed through Tom's head and made him shudder.

The air around him lit momentarily as faraway lightning shivered across the sky. Tom blinked – and when he looked again, the figure was gone. Shocked and confused, he stared and was still staring when a faint growl of thunder followed the flash. A drop of water fell fatly on his shoulder, then another and another.

He looked at the mill window, wanting to shout to Dad to come and see. But then he looked back at the wheel and changed his mind. There was nothing *to* see now; even the sense of dark menace had gone. Dad would just say it was his imagination, and maybe he was right.

Though Dublin and Katy wouldn't agree . . .

The leaves on the trees start to hiss as rain moved in up the valley, and suddenly the downpour began.

Tom turned and ran for the house.

2

Each time he passed by the water wheel over the next few days, Tom stopped and looked hard into the shadows; but there was nothing there. He didn't know whether to be relieved or disappointed. The incident had certainly shaken him, and he had no real wish to repeat it, but at the same time it was tugging at his curiosity; it was a mystery, and he wanted to solve it.

However, there were other demands on his time. The new school term was looming, which meant sorting out his new uniform and all the other dull but necessary things, and when he wasn't doing that, there was Dublin to consider. The puppy was definitely improving. He understood a few basic commands, even if he didn't often obey them, and he now walked on his lead without too much stopping and starting. His favourite route for walks was down the winding track that led through the valley to the creek. The creek, Tom thought, was a pretty amazing place; a long reach of smooth and surprisingly clear water, with a foreshore that was almost like a beach, and dense trees crowding down to the shore on both sides. There was a small stone jetty, and when the tide was low enough you could follow the foreshore for about half a mile before another path led up to the village.

Dublin loved the creek and tried every trick he could to get to the water. Sometimes he succeeded, and once he almost pulled Tom in with him before Tom had the sense to let go of the lead. He didn't worry too much; Dublin was a natural swimmer, and he always came back eventually, lolloping out on to the bank and shaking himself all over Tom's legs.

Term was only a few days away when the weather suddenly improved. It was typical, Tom thought: as well as having to get used to a new school, he would have the extra frustration of being stuck indoors while the sun shone outside. All he could do was make the most of it while he could, so he started taking Dublin to the creek more often. One gloriously warm afternoon he even speculated the prospect of swimming as they emerged from the trees at the creekside. But the thoughts abruptly vanished as he saw a small boat tied up beside the jetty. Someone was standing in the shallows, tilting the boat's outboard engine up out of the water, and Tom stopped, staring. It wasn't that he'd thought no one else ever came here. It was simply that, until now, he had never actually seen anyone, so this took him by surprise.

Then the person looked up, and he saw that it was a girl of about his own age, with short, curly dark hair. She was wearing old shorts and an older sweater, and she stared back, seemingly as surprised as he was.

Tom said, 'Hi.'

'Hi.' The girl's gaze shifted from him to Dublin. 'Lovely dog! How old is he?'

'Nearly five months.' Tom was encouraged. 'His name's Dublin, and he's an—'

'Irish wolfhound; I know.'

'Oh. Right.' Tom checked Dublin, who was straining on the lead. Dublin loved making new friends, but in his enthusiasm he would probably have knocked the girl backwards into the creek. The girl waded out of the water, came over and put a hand down to be sniffed. Dublin whined ecstatically, his entire rear end wagging, then rolled over and waved his paws in the air.

'He's completely daft,' Tom said.

'They usually are; it's in the breed.' She straightened up. She was almost as tall as he was, and seemed to be all angles. 'I'm Holly Blythe.'

'Right. Yeah. Tom McCarthy.'

She nodded briskly, as if to say, 'Well, that's got that out of the way.' Then: 'On holiday, are you?'

'No.' Tom felt slightly smug. 'We live here.' Then, being honest, he added, 'We've just moved in really; but it's great, I really like it, and—'

She interrupted him again, and suddenly her expression had changed. 'Moved in?' she echoed, an edge to her voice. 'Where?'

'Trevenna Mill. We—'

'Oh, I *see*. You're *that* lot, are you?'

'What?' Tom was perplexed; from a friendly – or at

20

least semi-friendly – manner she had switched in an instant to what looked and sounded like outright hostility. 'What do you mean, "that lot"?' he demanded.

She curled her lip. 'Townies, I suppose.'

'So what if we are?' Tom said indignantly. 'It's not a crime, is it?'

She snorted. 'Maybe it ought to be, with some people. I mean the sort who buy a piece of land and start putting up "keep out" notices, like they own the whole village.'

Tom's mental hackles were rising fast. 'We've put up *one*, and it says "private", not "keep out". Try learning to read!'

'Ha, ha. I don't need a degree to work out where *you're* coming from, do I? What are you planning to do – turn the mill into some cosy little suburban fortress, with burglar alarms, and a four-wheel drive that never gets dirty? That's *just* what we need!'

'Well, excuse me for breathing!' Tom tightened Dublin's leash with a jerk, pulling him away from Holly. 'I don't know what sort of chip you've got on your shoulder, but I've got better things to do than stand around listening to it! Come on, Dublin; we're going.' He started to walk away, then fired a last shot back over his shoulder. 'It's a good thing the rest of the people round here aren't like you. You'd empty the area in five minutes flat!'

He didn't wait to hear any retort she might have made but strode off, dragging the unwilling Dublin behind him. He didn't look back until they were a good way along the beach, and when he did he saw that she was pushing the boat back to deeper water and climbing in. He heard the engine starting up, and he sighed. *Stupid*. Why had she turned on him like that? It didn't make sense. And it had completely ruined his good mood.

'Come on, Dublin,' he said again. 'Let's go home.'

Dublin lifted one ear and looked at him with sorrowful eyes, as if he sympathized. Then he got up and, tail drooping, followed back towards the valley path.

Tom was still feeling sour when they arrived at the mill. Mum and Dad were hacking weeds in the garden, 'helped' by Katy, and as soon as Mum saw Tom's face she said, 'What's up?'

'Oh, nothing really.' Tom hunched his shoulders. 'I met this girl at the creek. She was OK at first, but then she suddenly started being rude and calling me a Townie.'

'Were you rude to her first?'

'No, I was not! I just said that we'd moved into the mill, and that set her off!'

'Ignore her,' said Dad. 'Best thing, with people like that.'

Mum shot him an old-fashioned look. 'What was her name, did she say?' she asked Tom.

Tom shrugged. 'Holly something . . . Blythe, I think.'

'The local vicar's called Blythe, isn't he?' said Dad. 'And he's got a daughter about Tom's age. Must be her.'

'Well, I'll be surprised if it is,' said Mum. 'I mean, you'd expect a vicar's child to be polite, if nothing else.' She would have expanded on the theme of why vicars' children should be expected to be polite, but at that moment Katy grabbed a handful of stinging nettles, got stung, and started yelling. Tom used the commotion to make his escape. He gave Dublin some food, left him wolfing it and wandered out again, round the other side of the house to the mill. Though he knew he should have shrugged off the encounter with Holly Blythe, he couldn't put it out of his mind. What was the matter with her? Everything had been fine until he'd mentioned the word Trevenna, then suddenly, wham, he was Public Enemy Number One. It didn't make any sense. He only hoped that she didn't go to the same school he was going to. That would about put the lid on it.

He mooched across the uneven grass, kicking at tussocks and feeling thoroughly ruffled. He wasn't consciously looking at the mill; it just happened that he glanced across to the water wheel –

And froze.

The hunched figure was on the stone ledge again. He could see it clearly, and it wasn't a trick of the light; nothing around the mill could possibly be casting a shadow of that shape. As before, he could make out no detail under its shrouding garments, but he had the awful feeling that unseen eyes were fixed on him, watching with an intensity that sent a cold shock through his veins.

Mouth dry, half hypnotized, Tom managed to find his voice. 'H . . . Hello . . . ?' It was a dumb thing to say, but he couldn't think of anything better. The shadow did not move, did not react in any way. But he still felt the stare, boring into him, unwavering.

'Look . . . I don't . . . I mean . . . what *are* you?' he quavered.

Nothing. Either it couldn't answer, or it didn't intend to, and suddenly he had the unaccountable feeling in his head of something laughing at him with silent malice.

Something close to panic welled up in Tom. 'Dad!' he shouted. 'Mum! Come here, *quick*!'

Footsteps thudded and Dad appeared, his face worried. 'Mum's still sorting Katy out. What's up?'

'Look!' Tom pointed. 'There, by the water wheel!'

Dad looked. 'What am I supposed to see?'

'What?' Tom's head turned. The figure had vanished.

'I —' He floundered, feeling as if all the stuffing had been knocked out of him. 'It was there just now; it . . .'

'What was?' Dad was eyeing him suspiciously, and suddenly Tom knew that he couldn't tell the truth. Thinking fast, he said, 'An — er — a rat, I think. But it was *huge*.'

'Oh.' Dad's face cleared. 'I haven't seen one before, but it's not surprising in a neglected old place like this. There's probably a whole colony of them in the mill building. Look, don't say anything to Mum, all right? I'll put down some bait or traps.' He grinned. 'Or maybe we can teach Dublin to catch them.'

'Yeah,' said Tom thinly. 'Right . . .'

'It couldn't have been a mink, could it?' Dad asked.

'What?'

'A mink. You know; they live wild in Britain now. They like water, and we *are* near a creek. If it was a mink, we ought to do something about it, because they kill a lot of other wildlife.'

'Oh,' said Tom. 'No, I . . . don't think it was.'

'Well, if you see it again, try to get a better look, to make sure.'

Tom thought: *I don't want to see it again. Whatever it was, I don't.* 'Yeah,' he said. 'Right. I will.'

Dad went away, leaving Tom gazing at the water wheel. No shadow, no hunched shape. But he had seen, and felt, *something*. He wondered briefly what Dublin would do if he was brought round to the millrace now. But though part of him was curious to find out, another and larger part didn't want to know. *Leave it alone*, he told himself. *Don't get involved*. It was better that way. It was safer.

He turned and headed back towards the house.

Tom didn't hate school, but he didn't particularly like it, either; it was just one of those burdens in life that had to be got through. All the same, when the new term began he was relieved to find that, as schools went, his new one

25

wasn't bad at all. And one big bonus was that Holly Blythe wasn't there.

Within a couple of weeks he had settled down to the routine, cheered, too, by the fact that because Easter was late this year the summer term wasn't going to be a long one. He made a few acquaintances, if not real friends, and the curriculum was pretty much what he was used to.

Back at home, work was progressing on the house and the mill. Mum had started researching the history of the place, and discovered that the mill itself had fallen out of use in the early nineteenth century. The last miller had apparently emigrated to New England with his family, and though the house was lived in after that, the mill had never been worked again. Dad had found the dried-up channel into which the stream had been diverted to turn the wheel, and traced it to the remains of an old sluice-gate that was used to control the flow of water.

'You never know,' he said enthusiastically one evening, 'we might be able to get the wheel going again one day. That would be something!'

'Sure,' said Mum. 'Did you see that pig that just flew past the window?'

'Well . . .' Dad grinned sheepishly. 'Maybe not. But it'd be fun to see how far we could get with restoring it. Oh, that reminds me – Tom, have you got any plans for this weekend?'

Tom looked up from where he was sitting on the floor pulling Dublin's ears in the way Dublin liked best. 'No-o,' he said cautiously. 'Why?'

'Good. I thought I'd have a go at that wall in the mill; you know, the one that looks as if it had a door behind it. Be interesting to see if it leads anywhere. Do you fancy giving me a hand?'

Tom didn't, really, but couldn't think of a ready excuse. 'Well . . .' he hedged.

'Great!' Dad knew him too well to give him time to wriggle out. 'You're booked for Saturday morning, then. Nine o'clock start!'

'No way! Eleven o'clock!'

'Ten,' said Dad.

Tom heaved a sigh. 'Ten-thirty?'

'Oh . . . all right. Though when I was your age—'

'I know,' said Tom. 'You had to get up at four o'clock every morning, work a sixteen-hour day *and* go to school for the other eight! Must've been a hard life in the Dark Ages!'

He dodged the cushion that Dad threw at him, and went back to playing with Dublin.

Saturday morning at eleven found a yawning Tom in the mill with a pair of old work gloves on, a chisel in his hand and a mallet in the other.

'Just chip round the old mortar gently, like this.' Dad showed him. 'Then see if any of these stones are loose enough for me to pull out. Watch your feet; if one fell out by itself and landed on your toe, you'd know it.'

'OK.' Tom nodded and swallowed another yawn. He would much rather have been in his bedroom with a computer game; that, after all, was what Saturday mornings were supposed to be for. But he had to admit to a sneaking interest in what Dad was doing. It *did* look as if there was once a door here, and they hadn't yet explored the part of the mill behind it, because there were no ground floor windows, only a gaping hole too high to reach safely from outside.

He got down to work, and for some while there was only the *tap-tap-tap* of the chisel, and some intermittent thumping and scraping as Dad worked on another part of the wall. Showers of mortar rattled down and soon littered the floor. The stuff was old and damp and came out easily, so that before long the stones stood proud and Tom thought that one of them, at least, might come out.

Dad came to have a look, and agreed. 'See the shape of them, the way they've been cut?' he said. 'You can tell now; they're different from the rest, probably newer. Right: let me get the crowbar and we'll see what happens. Stand back.'

Tom stood back as Dad levered at one of the largest stones. 'Yes!' he said. 'Here it comes . . .' The stone fell out with a thud that kicked up a cloud of dust, and Tom switched on his torch and peered into the hole that had been exposed.

'No door,' he said. 'There's a blank space, then another wall.'

'You sure?' Dad sounded disappointed.

'Certain. Look; you can see it.'

'Oh.' Dad stuck his head in the hole, shining the torch around. 'Well, that's weird. I really expected – hang on; there *is* something there. Lower down . . . oh blast, I can't see properly. We'll have to get some more stones out.' He reappeared with dirt and cobwebs in his hair, and picked up the crowbar again. 'Let's try this one.'

He prised at another block, near the base of the wall. As it began to shift outwards, Tom saw the stones above it sag. He knew what was going to happen, but only got as far as saying, 'Careful, Dad, the whole thing looks as if it—' when the entire section of wall gave way. Dad jumped back as the stones collapsed in a tumbled heap, and when the dust had cleared they both stared at what was revealed.

There was, as Tom had said, just another wall. It was about a metre behind the fallen one, forming a cavity, and at first they thought there was nothing else there.

Until they looked down at the piled earth and stone at their feet.

Tom told himself that it wasn't, and couldn't be, what it looked like. But then Dad said softly, 'Ye gods . . .'

He bent down, reaching, and Tom's voice came out in a sharp, high-pitched squeal. 'Dad, don't!'

But Dad had already grasped the end of the brownish-white shaft sticking out of the rubble. He pulled it free, and Tom's stomach turned over.

It was a long bone.

'Well,' said Dad, and his voice didn't sound too steady, either. 'I don't think we can put this down to Dublin . . .'

Tom swallowed. 'Wh . . . what do you think it is? Some sort of wild animal?'

'If it is, it's a big one; a deer at least, I'd have thought. Hang on; there are more, look.' Dad started to clear away earth with his hands. More bones appeared; another long one, a thinner one with a scimitar shape . . . then the top of something very smooth and curved began to emerge from the dirt.

Dad said a word that he didn't usually use in front of Tom. His fingers dug further into the debris, he felt carefully . . .

'I think,' he said, 'I'd better phone the police.'

Tom's heart turned over. 'Why? What is it?'

Dad pulled, and the thing he had found came free.

It was a human skull.

3

Tom, hovering as close as he was allowed, saw the police pathologist emerge from the mill with the senior detective. They were talking, but from this distance Tom couldn't hear what was being said. Dublin, beside him on a tight leash, flattened his ears and growled uneasily.

'Shh!' Tom said to the dog. But he understood how Dublin felt. Thoughts and fears were tumbling through his head. Whose were the bones? How had they got there? If it was a case of murder – and he had convinced himself that it was – would his own family be under suspicion? What if the police arrested Dad, or Mum, or even himself? What if—

Shut up! he told himself with silent ferocity. He was letting his imagination run riot. Of course they wouldn't be suspected. They'd only lived here for a few weeks, and those bones must have been lying in the mill for years. Unless—

The thought cut off as a uniformed policeman came out of the mill. He wore plastic gloves, and was carrying a large plastic bag. As he appeared, Dublin's head came up sharply; then suddenly he wrenched at his lead. Taken by surprise, Tom let go, and Dublin tore towards the mill, barking furiously.

'Dublin!' Tom raced after the dog and just managed to grab him before he could launch himself at the policeman. 'Sorry!' he gasped, dragging Dublin back. 'It was the bag – he saw it and went crazy!'

The pathologist, who had overheard, grinned. 'Natural instinct,' he said. 'He sees bones and he wants to bury 'em!'

Tom didn't think that was particularly funny, but the pathologist's friendly manner gave him the courage to ask, 'Can you tell anything about them yet?'

The pathologist glanced at the detective, who paused, then smiled faintly and nodded. 'Well, I doubt if you'll have to worry about a murder inquiry,' the pathologist told Tom. 'At a fair guess, I'd say they've been there for at least a hundred years.'

A huge surge of relief went through Tom and made him feel dizzy. 'Wow . . .' was the only reply he could think of.

'Quite,' said the pathologist dryly. 'Well, we'd better get finished up. If you can take your four-legged friend away before he starts eating the evidence . . .'

Tom dragged Dublin back to the house. Mum was in the sitting-room, distracting Katy, who was trying to get outside and see what the Funny Men were doing. One look at the bones and she would be having 'monter' nightmares all over again, Tom thought . . . and abruptly a memory clicked. A couple of weeks ago he had asked Katy what sort of 'monter' was at the mill. 'Sklington', she had said. *Skeleton.* And now, this. It was as if Katy had *known*.

'Tom?' Mum said. 'Any news?' She rolled her eyes towards Katy, warning him to be tactful.

'Oh – um, yeah.' Tom tried to push down the queasy feeling inside him. 'They reckon it's been there at least a hundred years, so there won't be any . . . well, you know.'

'That's a relief! Look, I'd better go and have a word with them. Keep an eye on Katy, will you? Whatever you do, don't let her follow me outside.'

'OK.' Tom was happy to stay in. Right at this moment he didn't want to go anywhere near the mill building.

The police left shortly afterwards, taking the bones with them. There would be a full forensic examination, they said, and they would let the McCarthys know the result in due course.

'It'll get into the papers, I suppose,' Dad said gloomily later, when Katy was in bed and they could talk more openly. 'We'll have queues of people coming to gawp.'

'It can't be helped,' said Mum. 'Anyway, you can hardly blame them. It's intriguing, a mystery – I mean, how on earth did a human body come to be walled up in the mill? It's positively mediaeval – the sort of thing that happened to nuns accused of being possessed by devils!'

'Trevenna's not mediaeval, is it?' Tom asked worriedly.

'No, of course it isn't,' said Dad. 'And even if it was, it's a mill, not a convent.'

'I think it was murder,' said Mum firmly. 'Well, it's logical, isn't it? If someone died naturally, they'd be buried in the churchyard, not shoved behind a stone wall and sealed up!'

'Unless they belonged to some weird religious sect,' Dad suggested. 'Or died of something so contagious that they had to be kept away from other people. Plague, for instance—'

'Oh, shut up!' Mum shuddered. 'That's gruesome!'

'No more gruesome than your murder theory. Anyway,' Dad yawned and stretched his arms, 'I expect we'll find out soon enough.'

We'll find out soon enough. Dad's words kept coming back to Tom as he lay in bed that night. He couldn't get to sleep for thinking about the bones, and he couldn't shake off the cold, uneasy feeling that had lodged itself in the pit of his stomach. Katy's 'sklington', the shadow hunching by the millrace, Mum's murder idea . . . they all tied in together somehow, and though he couldn't see a clear picture, he knew it would be there if just a few more pieces of the puzzle could be slotted together. But did he want to slot them together? Did he want to know any more, or did he just want to blot the whole thing out of his mind and pretend it had never happened?

Downstairs in the kitchen, which was directly below Tom's bedroom, Dublin whimpered in his sleep. He often did that, but tonight it seemed to Tom that there was something more meaningful about the noise. It sounded eerie, lonely, lost. He wished he had the courage to go downstairs and comfort the dog. He wished he had the courage to open his window, lean out and look at the mill. He wished he didn't have the ugly sensation that some invisible presence was observing him and silently laughing.

Tom did fall asleep, eventually. But his dreams were no more pleasant than wakefulness had been.

'So it's not really our province at all, but a matter for the historians and archaeologists.' The young detective finished his tea, smiled thanks at Mum and stood up. 'I don't doubt you'll have a steady stream of them coming to your door, not to mention the local media, so I'll leave you in peace and get back. And I'm sorry about all the upheaval, Mr McCarthy. But you understand, we had to go over the site thoroughly, to be sure.'

Dad nodded. 'It doesn't matter. The place was a complete mess to start with – in fact your guys have probably done me a favour. It'd have taken me weeks to demolish all that old stonework!'

'Well . . . at least you know there aren't any more skeletons in that particular cupboard.' The detective laughed at his own joke, then turned the laugh into a cough, said his goodbyes and went.

None of the McCarthys spoke until the sound of the car engine had faded away. Then Mum stood up, put the empty teacup in the sink and said softly, 'Two hundred years . . . Poor creature.'

Tom was thinking much along the same lines. The bones, they now knew, were those of a teenage girl or young woman, and the date of her death was somewhere around 1800. There was nothing to identify her, and it was impossible to be sure what she had died of. But the examination had revealed one strange thing. Many of the bones were broken – understandable enough, after such a long time. But it seemed they had been broken *before* her body was walled up. It looked as if she had had a terrible accident – or that Mum's murder theory was right.

'You know,' Mum said thoughtfully, 'there's a bit of a strange coincidence here.'

Tom looked up quickly, and Dad said, 'Is there? Why?'

'Well . . . when did the mill stop being worked?'

'Oh . . .' Dad saw what she was getting at. 'About two hundred years ago.'

'Right. And the last miller emigrated to America with his family, didn't he? So,' Mum started washing the teacup again, though she had already washed it once, '*why* did they leave?'

Dad raised his eyebrows. 'Running away from the scene of the crime, you mean? Mm. It makes sense.'

'You're saying maybe *they* killed her?' Tom asked.

'Yes,' said Mum. 'One of them, anyway. Or someone they knew and were trying to protect.'

'Perhaps they had a mad and dangerous son, who they kept chained up, and one night he got out and – *rrrAH*! Dad pulled a lunatic face and made clawing movements with his hands.

Mum wasn't impressed. 'You can laugh, but it's perfectly possible. Or maybe she was their daughter, and she fell in love with someone unsuitable, and there was a row, and it all got out of hand.' She was warming to her theme. 'Or she was a servant girl, and the miller murdered her because she resisted his amorous advances.' She saw Dad's expression. 'Well, you never know, do you?'

'Sounds like a bad romantic novel to me,' said Dad. 'I prefer the dangerous lunatic idea.'

'You would.' Mum looked at Tom. 'What do you think, Tom?'

Tom looked back at her. He wanted to say: 'I don't think it was any of those things. I think it was something much, much worse.' But he didn't. Skeletons and shadows and uneasy atmospheres . . . it *did* all tie together somehow, and the revelation about the broken bones added a new and even uglier dimension to it all. The girl's death hadn't been an accident, he was sure of that. Mum's murder theory made much more sense. But he didn't think that either Mum or Dad had come anywhere near guessing the real story.

Mum was waiting for him to answer, and abruptly an idea came to him.

'If you really want to find out,' he said, 'then why not

see if you can track down the miller's descendants?'

'What, in New England?'

'Yeah. If you can find out their name, and where they went, and when, we could do a search on the Internet.'

'Hey,' said Dad, 'this boy's got brains! He must take after me.'

Mum ignored him, but she was fired by Tom's idea. 'That's great!' she said enthusiastically. 'And the best place to look is the parish records. I want to talk to the vicar, anyway, so I can ask him about them.'

'Talk to the vicar?' Dad echoed. 'What for?'

'To ask him about giving that poor girl a proper burial, of course,' said Mum. Her eyes clouded a little. 'She's been waiting long enough, after all.'

That week was a busy one for Tom's parents. As the detective had predicted, the local media were very interested in the story, and the McCarthys had several visits from reporters, photographers, radio station interviewers and even a TV news crew. Tom was stuck at school and so missed most of it, but his classmates were fascinated, and he became a minor celebrity. Most teenagers would have revelled in the attention. Tom, though, just wished that the furore would die down as fast as possible.

Then, to his dismay, Mum insisted that they all went to church that Sunday.

'It's only fair,' she said. 'We can hardly go asking favours of the vicar if we never show up at his services, can we?'

'But I'm not religious!' Tom protested.

'Neither are Dad and I, particularly. But it shows willing.' Mum eyed him shrewdly. 'And if you do come face to face with his daughter, no public quarrelling, all right?'

'She started it, not me.'

'Whoever started it, it's not going to happen again. *Right*?'

Tom sighed. 'Right, Mum.'

So on Sunday they trooped along to Evensong. There weren't many people in the congregation, and Tom reckoned that nine-tenths of them were over eighty. Holly Blythe was there, sitting in the front pew with a woman who, he guessed, must be her mother. She saw him, but apart from exchanging one dirty look they ignored each other, and Tom sat, stood and knelt dutifully through the service. Katy, who had never been inside a church before, loved every minute and, apart from singing loudly in the wrong place two or three times, behaved herself very well.

Afterwards Mum towed everyone along to meet the vicar. The Reverend Blythe didn't fit Tom's mental picture of a vicar at all. He was sandy-haired, freckled, and built like a rugby prop-forward, and he had a booming laugh which sounded loud enough to rival the church bells. He didn't laugh, though, when Mum told him about the bones in the mill.

'I'd heard about it, of course,' he said, 'and I wanted to come over and see you about it. But . . . well, you know how it is; I didn't want to come putting my oar in, so to speak, if I wasn't wanted.' He smiled. 'You've solved my dilemma.'

He and Mum started to talk in earnest, and Tom wandered off to read gravestones, for want of anything more interesting. He had discovered one interesting epitaph to an Ezekiel Paynter, who had died at the age of ninety-four and was survived by seventeen children, forty-eight grandchildren and seventy-three great-great-grandchildren, when Mum and Dad came back down the path.

'Right!' said Mum, sounding pleased. 'It's all arranged. A search of the parish records, and a proper funeral for that poor girl. As soon as the pathology people release the bones, she'll be buried here in the churchyard.' Mum smiled. 'Then she can rest in peace.'

She and Dad walked on towards the lych gate, but Tom didn't follow at once. Instead he stood staring down at Ezekiel Paynter's gravestone. *Rest in peace*. Perhaps it was the answer. Perhaps, after the funeral, the eerie events at Trevenna Mill would finally come to an end.

He hoped so. He hoped it with all his heart.

The funeral was set for a Friday, and Tom felt powerfully and instinctively relieved. Since the bones were discovered, he had become more and more convinced that something was haunting the mill. Dublin now flatly refused to go anywhere near the millrace, and had grown strong enough to resist any attempt to force him to do anything he was determined not to. Tom sympathized. He hadn't exactly *seen* the figure by the race again, but he had felt a sense of its presence, or believed he had, several times. He also believed he knew, now, what it was. Because of its hunched shape, he had assumed it was an ancient crone. But the broken bones pointed to another possibility, and Tom felt sure that what he had seen was the ghost of the dead girl, crippled and twisted by her terrible fate. Perhaps she wanted justice, or even vengeance. Whatever the case, the funeral service would surely exorcise her, and the mill would be free of her influence.

The morning of the funeral – for which Tom had been excused school – began with a spectacular downpour. There wasn't any thunder or lightning, but the sheer volume of noise as rain hammered on the roof woke Tom far earlier than he would have liked.

'Rain before seven, fine before eleven,' his father assured him over breakfast. 'It'll stop before the service begins. You wait and see.'

He was right: by ten the rain was petering out, and by ten-thirty, when they set off for the church, it had gone. The ground was soggy underfoot, and there was a powerful wet smell in the air. As he got into the car, Tom heard Dublin howling inside the house, and a worm of disquiet moved in him. OK, Dublin often howled when he was left on his own. But this morning the noise seemed louder and more insistent, as if the dog was afraid rather than simply annoyed. Tom wished that the rain had not stopped him from taking his planned walk down to the creek with Dublin before the funeral began. It would have settled his nerves. As it was, he felt keyed-up, jumpy; like a bluebottle in a jam-jar, as his mother would have put it.

Oh, what the hell. Dublin was just being his usual self, and Tom was reading more into it than was there. Once this thing was over, life would get back to normal.

They parked in the village and walked to the church. The vicar had tried to keep publicity to a minimum: the village residents were naturally interested and had turned up in numbers, but Tom only recognized one reporter from the local paper. They shuffled into a pew; Katy, wide-eyed and eager, said loudly, 'Sing-song!' and Mum told her to shush or else.

The service wasn't a long one. Reverend Blythe had asked Mum and Dad if they would like any particular hymn, and Mum had chosen 'O God Our Help in Ages Past' because it seemed appropriate for someone who had died so long ago. The bones were in a miniature coffin in front of the altar rail; through the ceremony Tom kept finding his gaze drawn to it. So *small*. It was weird to think that a whole human being was in there, and as the vicar started to give a short address he tried not to look at the coffin again but to concentrate on something – anything – else.

The service neared its end. Reverend Blythe was using the old version of the prayer book, as would have been done in the nameless girl's lifetime. Listening to the words, Tom added a small prayer – well, sort of, he amended self-consciously – of his own, wishing her soul, if people had souls, good luck and peace. *You deserve it, after all this time*, he said silently. He felt a bit sick. The wet smell was still in his nostrils, and it seemed to have turned sour, like something decayed. Mum was affected by it, too; she kept wrinkling her nose distastefully, and sneezed twice. And one or two others in the next pew were shifting restlessly. A man leaned across to his neighbour to whisper something, and Tom heard the words, '. . . *bad eggs* . . .' The vicar coughed, frowned, coughed again.

Then suddenly the smell hit everyone like a solid wall.

It was a vile, overpowering stench, like mildew and rotting cabbage and burned hair all combined. Dad swore, forgetting where he was; several people started to get to their feet, and Katy wailed, 'Mumm-*eee*! Want to go home!'

Reverend Blythe looked quickly at the coffin, and Tom, struck and horrified by the same thought, looked too. But it couldn't be that. The coffin was sealed; and besides, the bones hadn't stunk when they were brought out of the mill, so why should they stink now?

'Ladies and gentlemen . . .' The vicar dropped the formal language he had been using. 'We seem to have a problem with the drains . . . I'm sorry about this dreadful smell, but I must ask you to bear with it for a minute or two longer. I'll complete the service as quickly as possible, and then we can all go outside.'

He rushed through the final part of the ceremony against a background of coughing and muttering, and the moment he had finished there was an undignified rush for the door.

'God almighty!' Dad said, gratefully gulping fresh air. 'What a stench! If that's the drains, they're going to need a bomb to clear them!'

Katy was crying, and Mum said to Tom, 'Can you sort her out and find her something to do? There's still the actual burial to come, and we can't have her causing a scene during that.' She pulled a face. 'Sorry, Tom.'

Truthfully, Tom was only too glad of the chance to get away from the church. He didn't want to see the burial; the fact that the bones were going to their final resting place was all he needed to know. He carried the wailing Katy out of the churchyard and across the road to the newsagent's, where he bought her an iced lolly. That cheered her up immediately; they went back to the churchyard and Tom sat on the low wall while Katy toddled off to look at a patch of wild flowers growing a short way off. He could see the group of people in the distance; the little coffin was lowered into the grave, then everyone turned slowly away.

'Flowers!' Katy's voice made him jump. 'Got some!'

She had reappeared, clutching a large bunch of white, bluebell-like flowers.

'Oh, no!' Tom was aghast. 'Kitten-Kat, they're wild flowers; you're not supposed to pick them! That's *naughty*!'

'Isn't,' Katy stated smugly. 'Nice flowers. Tom have them!'

She thrust the bunch into his hand, said, 'Go and find Mummy,' and ran off. Tom groaned and tailed after her, hiding the flowers behind his back before the vicar saw what had happened. Katy veered off to join the little procession walking along the path; Tom was about to follow when he had an idea. There was no one at the graveside now; he could put Katy's stolen flowers on the grave. No one else had left any, and it seemed an appropriate thing to do.

He crossed to the grave and looked down at it. It hadn't been deeply dug, and was already filled in; he could see the two grave-diggers walking away behind the congregation. Tom paused for a few seconds, thinking his own thoughts, then crouched down and laid the bunch of flowers on the soil.

'Rest in peace,' he murmured.

A voice behind him said, 'What are you doing?'

Tom straightened quickly, swung round, and came face

45

to face with Holly Blythe. She looked at the flowers, then glared coldly at him. 'Why are *you* putting flowers on the grave?'

Embarrassed and angered by the interruption of what had been a private gesture, Tom snapped back, 'Why shouldn't I? At least I bothered, which is more than you've done!'

He walked away before she could think of any retort, and didn't look back. Katy had found their parents, but Tom had been ruffled by Holly and wanted to calm down before he joined them. He walked towards the church again and cautiously put his head round the porch door. No smell. He sniffed again, to double check, then ventured further in. To his surprise the vile smell had gone completely, as if it had never existed. Yet it had been so overpowering . . . and as he remembered it, Tom abruptly recalled where he had smelled it before. It was the stink of stagnant water and decaying weed.

Just like the smell that sometimes hung faintly around the millrace.

4

In Tom's dream, Dublin was barking furiously. Tom cajoled and then shouted, but Dublin wouldn't stop. Eventually Tom's shouts became mixed with the dog's and he began to bark, too. Then suddenly he was awake, in his dark bedroom – and the noise was still going on.

'Dublin?' Tom sat up, blinking blearily. For a moment he thought the dog was with him in the room; then his head cleared and he realized that Dublin was downstairs, barking and yelping hysterically. What the heck –?

A bright bar showed under his door as the landing light was switched on, and footsteps came thudding. Tom leaped out of bed and opened the door in time to collide with Dad, who was wearing nothing but boxer shorts and holding a heavy torch in one hand. Mum came hurrying behind him, wielding a hairbrush, and the thing that should have occurred to Tom at once snapped into his mind.

He said in alarm, 'Burglars?'

'Could be.' Dad headed for the stairs, with Mum behind him, and Tom followed. As they reached the hall they could hear Dublin hurling himself against the kitchen door; Mum switched more lights on, while Dad let Dublin out. The dog shot past like a cannonball, still barking madly, and Tom grabbed an umbrella from the hall stand as Dad opened the front door. He expected Dublin to hurtle into the garden, but instead he started to race in circles round and round the hall.

'Find 'em, Dublin!' Tom urged. 'Go get 'em!'

Dublin took no notice, but carried on circling. Dad was shining the torch around outside, but there were no running footsteps or sounds of a car engine starting up. Nor, when they all searched the ground floor, was there any trace of an intruder. No windows or doors open, no sign of trouble at all.

Eventually they calmed Dublin down, though it took nearly ten minutes.

'I don't know what could have got into him,' said Mum when all was quiet at last. 'He's never done anything like that before.'

'Maybe he scented a cat or something outside?' Dad suggested. 'It might have set him off; then we came down and that only made him more excited.'

'It's possible,' Mum agreed. 'But if he's going to do that too often, he won't be very popular with me!'

Tom rubbed Dublin's chest, and Dublin rolled over blissfully, begging for more. 'Can I have him in my room for the rest of tonight, Mum?' he asked.

'No!' said Mum. 'He'll think he only has to bark himself stupid to be allowed on your bed, and he'll start doing it every night! Leave him where he is, and let's all go back upstairs.'

Katy, miraculously, had slept through the whole thing, and there wasn't a sound from her room as Tom and his parents said goodnight. Yawning, and wondering again what had started Dublin off, Tom went into his room. In his hurry he hadn't turned the light on, so the only illumination came from the half moon outside his window. Vaguely his brain registered the dim outlines of his bed, chest of drawers, computer work-station . . .

And something else, that shouldn't have been there.

Tom's mind wasn't working at full speed, so it took a second or two before the fact dawned. When it did, he stopped and stood rigid, as though a violent electric shock had gone through him.

There was someone else in the room.

Alarm hit Tom like a sledgehammer blow, and he opened his mouth to yell. But before he could utter a sound, the indistinct figure raised a finger to its lips, warning him to silence. He was so stunned that the yell died in his throat, and all he could do was stand staring, like a mesmerized rabbit, at the intruder. A girl – he couldn't see her face clearly in the dimness, but she was young; maybe only a year or two older than himself. She was wearing a long dress with an apron over it, and her hair was caught back in a kind of linen cap, in the style of another century . . .

The girl held something out to him, and a light voice, with a strong Cornish accent, seemed to come from a great way off.

49

'My name is Susannah. You placed these for me. Thank you for your kindness.'

The object she was holding fell to the floor. Instinctively Tom's gaze followed it; then a second instinct made him look quickly up again.

The girl had vanished.

Tom's jaw dropped, and the mesmerized rabbit became a stranded fish as he gaped blankly at the empty space where she had been standing. His racing thoughts said: *Imagination! Hallucination! I'm still asleep!* But when he looked down at the floor again, he knew it was none of those things.

A white, bluebell-like flower lay near his feet. It was drooping, as if it had been picked some hours ago and not put in water. Tom knew at once that it must – could only – be from Katy's bunch. The bunch that he had laid on the grave this morning.

He had come face to face with the Trevenna Mill ghost.

Tom didn't get much more sleep that night. For an hour or more he lay in bed, keyed-up, as he wondered if the girl in the old-fashioned clothes would return. She didn't; and at last the tension of waiting became too much to bear, so he tried to think about something else. That, though, proved impossible. His mind kept turning back to the dim figure, and over and over again he relived the encounter, wondering what it meant.

The one certain thing was that it had not been a dream. The flower was proof of that – he had put it on his bedside table, and he only had to turn his head to see it there, as real and solid as he was. Dublin's outburst, too, was explained. He must have sensed the ghost's presence, and that was what had set him off.

The knowledge that he had actually encountered a ghost sent a squirming sensation over Tom's skin. But apart from the shock she had caused, there had been nothing frightening about her. Quite the opposite, in fact. She had told him her name, Susannah, and the feeling he had had from her was, if anything, one of friendship. Why, though, had she vanished so abruptly? More to the point, why had she appeared at all? In theory the funeral should have released her and set her at rest; that was the general idea of such things, wasn't it? Perhaps, Tom thought, she had simply made one last visit to Trevenna, as a kind of thank you and farewell? It was the only explanation he could come up with. But somehow he had the feeling that it wasn't quite the answer.

Eventually he fell asleep again. When he woke it was daylight and he could hear Katy chattering to Mum in the kitchen below him. He looked at his bedside table. The flower was still there, and he laid it between the centre pages of the biggest book he had, to press and preserve it. Susannah's flower. He wanted to know more about her: who she was, when she had lived, how she had died. Though part of him wanted to believe it, he couldn't convince himself that she was really and truly gone. He wanted to see her again, talk to her if he could, and learn her story. Was it possible? And if it was, how could it be done?

He dressed and went down to breakfast. It was desperately tempting to tell Mum and Dad everything, but logic said no. After all, why should they believe a word? He had no evidence except for the flower, and to them that wouldn't prove anything. However much he wanted to share this and talk about it with someone, it just wasn't possible.

He hung around the mill all morning, irrationally hoping that Susannah might put in another appearance. She didn't; and in the afternoon Tom gave up and took Dublin for a long walk. At the creek the tide was low, and they went upstream as far as they could along the shore, only turning back when clouds began to gather. The rain started when they were still a mile from home, but Tom was too preoccupied to mind much. An idea had occurred to him, and though it seemed crazy, there was an outside chance that it could work. If he went to Susannah's grave when no one else was around, and talked to her, maybe she might hear him . . . ?

They had reached the path that led back to Trevenna Mill, but after a thoughtful pause Tom continued along the creek shore instead. Dublin was surprised and started to pull on his lead. He wanted to go home, where there would be food and a delectable rubdown with an old towel.

'No,' Tom told him, giving the lead a firm tug. 'Walk.' The rain would keep people indoors; no one would see him in the churchyard. 'We're going to the village.'

Dublin eyed him reproachfully, then made a whining sound that Tom took to be a sigh, and walked on with his ears drooping.

The rain was falling more heavily and the churchyard looked as deserted as Tom had hoped. He led Dublin through the lych gate and headed for Susannah's grave. When it came in sight, though, he had an unpleasant surprise. Someone else was already there. And though she was crouching down with her back to him, he knew immediately that it was Holly Blythe.

He would have turned round and walked away before she noticed him, but then he saw that she had taken the flowers – *his* flowers – from the grave and was fiddling with them. Indignantly he strode towards her.

'Hey!' he called when he was close enough. 'What do you think you're doing?'

She looked round, startled, and got to her feet as he reached her, looking defensive and aggressive at once. 'It's none of your business,' she said.

'It is if you're messing around with my flowers! Leave them alone!'

A smile that was more of a sneer appeared on her face. 'OK. If you want them to die because they're not in water, that's fine with me. I'll just put *my* flowers in the jam-jar and leave you to sulk on your own!' She glanced at the dog and added with pointed pleasantness, 'Hello, Dublin.'

Tom saw then that there was a jam-jar of water by the grave. His own flowers were in it, and Holly had been adding more: some tulips and a sprig of early honeysuckle.

'Oh . . .' he said.

'Yeah, "oh". So next time, try getting the facts before you climb on your high horse, right? Anyone'd think you had some sort of right over the grave! You don't even know who she was!'

Tom didn't know why he did it, but the impulse came and the words were out before he could stop them. 'I know more about her than you do!' he retorted.

Holly sneered again. 'Oh, sure! Like what?'

'Like her name. She was called Susannah.'

There was a sharp silence. Holly stared at him. Then after a couple of seconds she said, 'What do you mean?'

'Just what I say. Her name was Susannah.'

Another pause. 'How can you *possibly* know something like that?' Holly demanded.

It was a challenge, and Tom was so annoyed by it that he threw caution to the winds. He looked her straight in the eye and replied, 'Because she told me, when I saw her in my room last night.'

Holly laughed out loud, and his reckless impulse collapsed instantly. *Oh, no, he thought, what have I done? Idiot, idiot, idiot – to blurt it out to HER, of all people –*

Then suddenly the laughter stopped as Holly took in the expression on his face. She stared at him, very hard. Then she said, 'You're serious . . . aren't you?'

The change in her voice was so great that Tom was thrown. He eyed her warily, then shrugged. 'Yeah. I am.'

She swallowed as if something had stuck in her throat. 'Then it's true. There *is* a ghost at the mill . . .'

'What? You mean, you *knew*?'

Holly shook her head. 'Not for sure. But I've had a feeling for ages that the place was, well . . .'

'Haunted?'

A nod this time. 'I used to go up there a lot. Not to do anything especially, just look around. I never actually *saw* anything – at least, I don't think I did; though there was one time . . . But I got a feeling about it.' She hesitated, and a frown appeared, creasing her eyebrows together. 'Then you moved in, and I couldn't go any more.'

'Oh, I *see*.' This suddenly explained her attitude, and Tom found himself almost wanting to laugh. 'That's why you went for me that day by the creek, is it? All that stuff about Townies – you were just riled because we'd come along and spoiled your fun!'

Her face reddened and the hostile look came back.

55

'Well, if you want to be rude about it—'

'OK, OK.' Tom held up both hands in a peace gesture. 'I'm sorry, I shouldn't have said it that way. Look . . . can we start again? This thing about Susannah's got to be more important than quarrelling. We're the only ones who even know about it.'

She was surprised. 'You haven't told anybody else?'

'No. Just you. And I only did that because you were getting my back up and coming over all superior.'

She smiled faintly, gazing at the ground and scuffing one foot. 'Sorry. Dad says it's my worst habit.'

'Well, maybe for once it was a good thing.' Tom paused. 'I want to find out more about Susannah. I could do with some help.'

Holly raised her head slightly. Water dripped from the ends of her hair. 'Yeah?'

'Yeah.'

'So you're saying . . .' She was still cautious, not wanting to be the first to suggest it. So Tom jumped in.

'I'm saying, what about *you* helping me?'

He waited for what seemed like an eternity, while Holly looked at the ground again. Then at last:

'Look . . . have you got to get back yet?' she said.

'No.'

'Right. You see . . . I've got something at home. Some photos I took at the mill, ages ago. It's weird, because . . . well, why don't you come back with me and see it for yourself?'

Tom felt a quick stir of excitement. 'OK!' he said.

She hesitated again, then suddenly looked up and gave him the first genuine smile he'd ever seen from her. 'Come on, then. It's got to be better than standing around here getting soaked!'

If the Reverend Blythe was surprised to see Holly and Tom together, he didn't show it. He said hello to Tom, asked after his family, then retreated to his study to work. Holly hung up their dripping coats, took Tom into a small but cosy sitting-room, then ran upstairs and came down again with a cardboard box.

'They're in here somewhere.' She dumped the box on a low table and started to rummage. Papers, notebooks and other bits and pieces spilled all over the place, until finally she pulled out a small bundle of photos.

'I got a camera for my birthday last year, and I wanted to try it out,' Holly explained. 'So I went up to the mill and took a load of shots. I didn't see anything funny at the time, but when the film came back from the chemist, I found these.'

She handed Tom two of the photos. The first was a picture of the old mill house, with the water wheel to one side. For a moment Tom couldn't see anything odd about it. But then he saw a peculiar smudge, just behind and to the right of the wheel. It was a darkish grey, almost like smoke, and its shape was oval-ish and very regular.

He looked at the other picture. This one showed the overgrown garden, with the valley wood beyond it. There was another smudge at the edge of the trees, the same grey colour but a different shape. If Tom squinted, it looked vaguely like a human being, running . . .

'Dad said light must have got into the camera,' Holly said. 'But I've seen pictures where that's happened, and they don't look the same at all.'

Tom nodded. He looked at the mill photo again and felt his heart start to beat more quickly. 'When we were in the churchyard, you said you never actually saw anything at the mill, except for one time. Was it when you took this picture?'

'No,' said Holly. 'It was another time. And I didn't really *see* it. It was more a feeling I had, as if something was watching me.'

'Where did it happen?'

She nodded at the photo. 'Right there, by the millrace. That's why I was freaked when I saw the smudge.' She saw Tom's expression. 'Why? Have you – ?'

'Yes. In exactly the same place. I felt it, too. And I definitely saw something.'

He told Holly about his eerie experience, about Katy's 'monter' comment and about Dublin's absolute refusal, now, to go anywhere near the millrace. Then he told her in detail what had happened last night. When he finished, Holly whistled softly.

'A real ghost . . . Whoo!' For a moment she looked

dubious. 'Look, you're not winding me up, are you? This really did happen?'

'Cross my heart,' said Tom. 'She was there, and I was wide awake. I kept the flower she dropped. I've pressed it in a book, if you want to see it.'

'I'd like to. So that other thing – the figure by the millrace – you think that was her?'

'It must have been, mustn't it? The thing is, now that her bones have been properly buried, shouldn't she . . . well, be at rest, or whatever? Your dad's a vicar; you should know about that sort of thing.'

'You mean, you don't think she is at rest? She might have appeared in your room just to say thanks and goodbye.'

'I thought that, and I suppose it makes sense. But . . .' Tom fished for an explanation and couldn't find it, so all he could add was, 'I've just got a feeling that there's more to it. She seemed . . . unsettled, somehow.'

Holly looked at Dublin, who had gone to sleep on a rug near their feet. 'What about him? Is he OK about the wheel now or does it still freak him?'

'I haven't tried taking him near it.'

'Then maybe you should. Animals can sense things we can't – like the way you said he woke you up last night, when Susannah was around.'

It was a good idea, and Tom agreed. 'If she is gone . . .' he said, and grinned sheepishly. 'I don't know . . . it's going to be a bit of a disappointment, isn't it?'

'Yes,' Holly admitted. 'Though there's still a lot more to find out. Such as when she lived. And how she died.'

He nodded, sobered by that thought. 'It's Sunday tomorrow,' he said. 'No school. Why not come up to the mill? If you want to, that is. We could start exploring.'

'I'd like that. It'll have to be after morning service, though.' She pulled a face. 'When you're the vicar's daughter there's no escape. About half-past eleven?'

'Great. Stay for lunch. Mum won't mind.' *I hope*, Tom added to himself. 'And bring the photos. I'd like to have another look at them.'

The rain had eased off, so Tom wasn't much wetter than he had already been by the time he and Dublin got back to Trevenna Mill. As he opened the gate, Tom looked at the mill building looming ahead of him. He wasn't sure if he wanted to try out Holly's suggestion. If Susannah *was* truly gone, it would, as he had said, be disappointing in a way. But it had to be tested some time. So why not get the answer now, rather than keep on guessing?

He tugged on Dublin's lead. 'Come on. We'll go round this way.'

Dublin followed happily enough as Tom led him towards the mill. His parents weren't anywhere in sight, but the kitchen light was on and Tom could hear a radio playing what sounded like a sports commentary. 'Come on, Dublin,' he said again. Round the side of the mill, towards the wheel and the race and—

Dublin stopped so suddenly that it jerked Tom's arm in its socket. He turned. The dog was standing rigid, staring at the millwheel, his tail between his legs.

'Dublin? Come on, boy. There's nothing there now.' *Is there . . . ?*

Dublin growled. He was staring fixedly at the wheel. Then the growl became a snarl, and then a bark, and before Tom could collect himself, Dublin yanked the lead out of his hand, spun round and raced away towards the house as if a hundred demons were snapping at his heels.

5

The worst of the rain cleared overnight, and by morning it was only showery with bouts of sunshine in between. Mrs McCarthy was surprised when Tom told her that Holly was coming to visit, but she managed not to ask too many embarrassing questions and said, yes, certainly she could stay to lunch.

Holly arrived at eleven forty-five, appearing, to Tom's surprise, from the valley path. As Dublin leaped all over her, making muddy pawprints on her clothes and licking her face as if she was an enormous dog-biscuit, Tom said, 'How did you get round that way? The tide's wrong for walking, isn't it?'

'I came by boat,' she told him.

'Oh! That one I saw you with the first time, when we— well, never mind. Is it yours, then?'

'No; it belongs to someone in the village, but he lets me borrow it. That's enough, Dublin; get down, good boy!'

Tom hauled Dublin off and Holly wiped her face. She grinned. 'I really enjoyed coming through the gate with the "private" notice on it.'

Tom flushed but decided to ignore the tease. He had something much more important to say, and nodded at the wriggling dog. 'I tried to take him to the water wheel when I got home yesterday.'

'Oh? And what . . . ?' She read his expression. 'Ah. Same reaction?'

He nodded. 'Exactly the same. She's still there. Or something is.'

Holly's eyes narrowed. 'What does that mean?'

Tom had done a lot of thinking overnight, and something that had been nagging at him was now clearer in his mind. 'One thing doesn't add up,' he said. 'When Susannah appeared in my room, I wasn't scared. Shocked, sure; anyone would be. But not *scared*. She was . . . well, friendly, is the best word for it, I suppose. But whatever it is that's hanging around the mill doesn't feel friendly at all. And when you add in what Katy said, and how Dublin behaves –'

'You think whatever's there might not be Susannah?'

'It's only a theory. But it makes a weird kind of sense.'

Holly studied the mill with narrowed eyes. 'I'd like to get over that bridge and take a look at the far side.'

'Not a chance,' Tom told her. 'Dad's put an absolute ban on anyone going on the bridge; it's so rotten it would probably collapse under Katy's weight, never mind ours.'

'We could climb down into the race. Got a couple of ladders?'

'Probably, but if Dad or Mum saw us they'd go through the roof.'

'We'll have to wait till they're not around, then.' Holly dismissed his doubts airily. She seemed completely unfazed by the idea of exploring around the wheel, but though he didn't want to admit it, Tom wasn't at all keen. It wasn't the safety problem. It was an illogical but unshakeable feeling that to go over there and start poking around would be very, very foolish.

Wanting to steer Holly away from the idea, he said, 'We can't do it today, anyway. What about Susannah? I really want to find out more about her, but I don't even know where to start.'

Holly was still watching the mill. 'The best person to tell us, of course, would be Susannah herself. And you know what? I think she's still around.'

'Why?'

'I don't know. It's just an instinct.' She turned away from the mill and seemed to be weighing something up in her mind. At last she faced him. 'When I used to come up here, I kept getting the feeling that I wasn't alone. It happened a lot; and sometimes it was so strong that it really unnerved me. I tried calling out: you know, the old "Hello, is there anybody there?" routine. There was never any answer. But it was as if someone had heard me, and they *wanted* to answer, but couldn't for some reason.' She shrugged. 'Sounds crazy, I know. But that's what it was like.'

'Can you feel anything like that today?' Tom asked eagerly.

'After what we've been talking about, it'd be all too easy to imagine it, wouldn't it? But . . . yes. I think I can. I think Susannah isn't far away.'

Tom stared around at the quiet garden, the sunlit house, the silent mill. He could feel nothing, and he said, 'Do you know where?'

'No. Just around; I can't be any more accurate than that.'

'Can ghosts appear in the daytime?'

'Why not? Think about the photo I took. That was in broad daylight.'

'Yes . . . yes, it was.' He glanced towards the house. 'I wonder what would happen if we called to her now? Two of us might stand a better chance of . . . well, getting through.'

'I thought that, too. But we'd better not do it in earshot of your mum and dad, or they'll think we're demented.' Holly thought for a few moments, then: 'Let's go into the mill. The place where you found the bones. If she's tied to any special spot, it should be there. Anyway, I'd like to see it.'

Tom pushed down an irrational shiver. 'All right.' He looked down at Dublin. 'What about him?'

'Is he scared of the mill building?'

'He doesn't seem to be. It's just the wheel.'

'Then I think we should take him with us, and see what he does. If Susannah does try to answer us, he'll probably be the first one to sense her.'

Dublin was happy enough to go with them, and they walked towards the mill door. Tom thought: *This is unreal. It's a sunny Sunday morning, and I'm heading for an old ruin to try to make contact with a ghost.* But he said nothing, and firmly pushed down the slightly queasy sensation that was trying to take control of his stomach, as they ducked under the lintel and entered the gloomy interior.

'Wow.' Holly straightened up and looked around, peering in the dismal light. 'What a creepy place!'

'Haven't you been in here before?'

'No, it was all boarded up when I used to come.' She scratched at the wall, and dust and small flakes of stone scattered down. 'Where did you find the bones?'

'Over there.' Tom pointed to the excavated section. 'Where it looks as if there used to be a door. The police did a lot more digging, but they didn't find anything else.'

He followed her to the spot, keeping an eye on Dublin. The dog didn't seem particularly interested; he sniffed at one or two piles of rubble, then sat down and started to scratch one ear with a hind foot. Holly looked from floor to ceiling, her face sombre. Then she said quietly.

'Do you think Susannah could still have been alive when she was put in here?'

'God, I hope not!' Tom was horrified by that macabre idea, and denied it hastily. 'She can't have been. So many of the bones were broken – she must have died of her injuries, not . . .' He waved a hand at the wall, unwilling to say the rest, then added, 'Whatever made you think of a gruesome thing like that?'

'I was just considering possibilities,' said Holly. 'If we could guess at what happened to Susannah, and say so when we try to contact her, it might make her more willing to answer.' She gave her little shrug again. 'Only a thought.'

'Well, don't think things like that to me! I live here, remember. I don't want that sort of image going round in my head when I'm lying in bed at night!'

'Sorry.' Holly smiled faintly. 'That's made the party go with a bang, hasn't it? Well done, Holly. Remember to engage brain before operating mouth.' She let out her breath in a rush. 'Come on. Let's try and call her.'

'OK.' Again Tom pushed down the queasy feeling. 'How do we do it?'

'Just talk to her, I suppose. Tell her who we are, and that we want to know more about her. And that we want to help, if we can.'

He nodded. For several seconds there was silence. Then:

'Susannah.' Holly spoke quietly. 'Susannah, are you here? My name's Holly, and this is Tom. He lives at the mill now.' She rolled her eyes in Tom's direction, prompting him to say something.

'Er . . . hello, Susannah,' he ventured. 'I saw you last night.' He paused. 'I've pressed the flower.'

At the edge of his vision he saw that Dublin had stopped scratching and was watching them. Did it mean anything? Had the dog sensed some change that they weren't aware of?

'Susannah,' said Holly, 'we'd like to talk to you. We want to know more about you. Please answer us.'

No response. Dust motes drifted on a shaft of sunlight, and Tom felt as if he could have reached out and touched the silence. Dublin yawned, then settled down and laid his head on his outstretched front paws.

'She isn't here,' said Tom.

'Shh!' Holly waved at him to be quiet. 'I thought I felt something.'

Invisible spiders crawled up Tom's spine. He looked uneasily around at the gloomy scene, but his mind couldn't pick up anything strange. Except . . .

He shivered suddenly, and hissed, 'It's getting cold in here!'

'I know,' Holly whispered back. She bit her lip. 'When she came to you last night, did it turn cold then?'

'No.' He remembered clearly. 'Definitely not.'

'Right.' Holly was looking nervous now. 'I think maybe we ought to go outside.'

Tom got as far as, 'Why? What—' when Dublin suddenly sprang to his feet and growled. He was staring deeper into the building, past the demolished wall to the area where the mill machinery had once creaked and rumbled.

'What's he seen?' Tom's voice went up the scale to a squeak.

'I don't know.' Holly backed a pace towards the door. 'But I think we ought to go.'

Tom would never know what made him look over his shoulder then. Instinct, a flash of premonition; or maybe it was sheer coincidence. But he did look, and what he saw made him yelp aloud. Susannah's face was at one of the gaping window holes, looking in at them.

Their eyes met, and with a rapid, emphatic shake of her head Susannah dodged out of sight. Holly had spun round at Tom's cry, but she wasn't in time to see what he had seen.

'Tom!' she shouted as he ran for the door. He ignored her, and she raced after him. Dublin saw them go and raced too, barrelling through the doorway and nearly sending Holly flying as he tore outside.

Tom was looking wildly around at the garden. 'What is it?' Holly gasped, catching up. 'What happened?'

'It was her! Susannah – she was here, looking in at the window!' Tom's gaze swept the garden again. 'But she's vanished.'

'Which way did she go, did you see?'

He shook his head. 'She saw me and just *went*. As if she was frightened.'

'Dublin!' Holly bent to the dog, grasping his muzzle between her hands. 'Where's Susannah? Find, boy. Find!'

Dublin whined and wriggled. He knew 'find' but

obviously had no idea what she expected him to look for. Holly sighed and straightened. 'He can't sense her. Look, Tom, are you sure you really saw her?'

'Of course I am!' Tom snapped.

'OK, OK; don't blow up, I believe you. It's just weird . . .'

'What is?'

'You said she was out here. And Dublin started growling just before she appeared. But whatever upset him was *inside* the mill.'

She was right. Tom looked uneasily back at the building, then at Dublin. The dog seemed perfectly all right now. But it had been a different story a few moments ago.

He walked back to the mill and went cautiously inside. It didn't feel so cold now, but all the same he couldn't suppress a shiver as he looked into the quiet, still depths of the building.

'Susannah . . . ?' he ventured. The only answer was a faint echo of his own voice.

'It's gone,' said Holly from behind him. She, too, had stepped through the door. 'Whatever freaked Dublin, it isn't here any more.' She hunched her shoulders and rubbed her own arms. 'And it wasn't Susannah. I think your theory's right. There's something else haunting this place, as well as her.'

'But what?' Tom asked uneasily.

'That's what we're going to have to find out.'

He nodded. 'This is going to sound daft, but . . . when I saw Susannah just now, she shook her head at me. I'm sure it meant something. Like a . . . a . . .'

'A warning?'

'That's it. That's it *exactly*. I mean, I might be wrong, but –'

'No,' said Holly. 'I don't think you are.' She paused. 'Your mum's been trying to find out about the people who lived here in Susannah's time, hasn't she? How far has she got?'

'Last I heard, not very. She was going to see if she could track down their descendants in the States, but I don't know if she's started on that yet.'

'Maybe we ought to talk to her at lunchtime. Not tell her about what's just happened, of course, but see if she's come across anything we could find useful.' Holly frowned in the gloom. 'Because I've got a theory, too. Whatever this . . . *thing* is, I reckon it might have something to do with Susannah's death. In fact, I think it might have *everything* to do with it.'

As the McCarthys and Holly sat eating roast chicken at the kitchen table, Tom asked Mum about her research. Disappointingly, she hadn't made a great deal of progress; although, she said, she had discovered that the name of the last miller's family was Hoskin. John Hoskin had married a woman called Mercy Carter in 1798, and seven Hoskin children had been baptized in the following twelve years.

Tom felt his pulse quickening. 'What were the children's names?' he asked.

'They're in the register of course, but I can't remember them all,' said Mrs McCarthy. 'There was a Ruth, I think; and a Samuel . . . or was it Daniel?'

Tom opened his mouth to say, 'Was there a Susannah?' but Holly kicked his ankle under the table and shot him a warning look.

'Anyway, there were four girls and three boys,' Tom's mother went on. 'But of course we can't know if any of them was *her*.'

'And did they emigrate, Mrs McCarthy?' Holly asked.

'Well, there aren't any more Hoskins in the births or deaths register after the last child's baptism, so it certainly looks as if they left the village. But I couldn't find anything that told me exactly when and where they went.'

'We know it was somewhere in New England, don't we?' Tom put in.

'Ye-es,' his mother agreed. 'But that's a *very* big area. Still, like you said the other day, it might be worth trying the Internet, to see if we can trace any descendants.'

'Sure,' said Tom, aware that Holly was looking at him very intently. 'I'll see what I can do.'

'Only when the phone rate's cheap,' Mr McCarthy warned. 'If I get an enormous bill—'

Tom was saved from replying by Katy, who chose that moment to hurl a roast potato across the kitchen. It ricocheted off the fridge door and landed in Dublin's basket, right in front of his nose. Dublin gobbled the potato, Mum ticked off Katy, Katy had a tantrum, and by the time calmed reigned again the subject had been dropped. As soon as the meal was finished, and Mrs McCarthy had declined Holly's offer to help with the washing-up, Tom and Holly went outside again.

'Hoskin,' Holly said thoughtfully as they stood looking at the mill. 'It's a start, isn't it?' She began to walk slowly towards the corner of the old building. 'I wonder if Susannah's watching us now? If she can hear us?'

Tom looked quickly over his shoulder, but there was no flicker of movement, no glimpse of a shadowy figure. Holly disappeared round the corner of the mill and after a minute he followed, to find that she had climbed the bank to the stone bridge support, and was staring at the rotting water wheel with a frown on her face.

'What's the connection?' she said as he came up to join her. 'If there *are* two hauntings here, there's got to be some link between them. What is it?'

She was asking questions that Tom couldn't answer, and he turned away, kicking at a grass tussock and sending up a spray of water from the last rain-shower. 'If you ask me,' he said, 'Susannah isn't going to tell us. In fact, I don't think we'll get her to talk to us again. I don't know why, but I've got this feeling that she said all she's going to that first time, when I saw her in my room.' Holly didn't answer, and he went on, 'Unless we can come up with some new strategy, I don't think we'll learn anything from her. Any ideas?' Still Holly didn't answer, and after a moment he said, 'Did you hear me? I asked—'

The words broke off as he turned his head. Holly was motionless, staring fixedly at the ledge on the far side of the millrace.

And on the ledge, in the shadow of the wheel, crouched a dark, hunched shape.

'Holly!' Tom hissed. 'That's it! The thing I saw before!'

Holly ignored him; in fact she didn't seem to have heard. She started to move, in a curious, sidling way that took her towards the decayed footbridge. Her gaze didn't leave the ledge for a moment. And the thing in the shadows seemed to be watching her in its turn.

'*Holly!*' An intuitive disquiet welled in Tom. 'Holly, stop! Stay there, don't go near the bridge!'

She stopped, wavered. 'I . . . don't want to . . .' she said in a quavering voice, 'but . . .' She took another step, and Tom's disquiet swelled to alarm.

'But what?' he shouted. 'What's the matter?'

On the ledge, the shadow-figure shifted. 'I can't . . . stop myself,' Holly said fearfully. 'It's as if something's . . . *making* me go, and I can't stop!'

She was almost at the bridge. Tom ran to her and grasped hold of her arm to pull her back. She resisted, trying to shake his hands off, and for several seconds they swayed and slithered together on the wet grass in a weird kind of silent fight. He could feel something dragging at his mind, compelling him to look at the ledge again, but he shut his eyes against the compulsion. Holly was as tall as he was, and strong; she took another step towards the bridge, dragging him with her—

Behind them, a voice called shrilly, '*No!*'

Tom let go of Holly in his shock, and they reeled off balance. Susannah was standing at the edge of the garden. She looked as real and solid as they were; her expression was distraught and she held up both hands, palms outward, towards the millwheel, as though to push something away.

Tom felt the mental backlash as the spell on Holly snapped. Holly staggered, almost fell, righted herself, and stared, stunned, at the girl in the old-fashioned dress.

'Susannah . . .?' she gasped. Susannah tensed at the sound of her name. Then she made another gesture, a single, sweeping jerk of one arm that warned them clearly to get away from the millrace. Tom jerked his head round to glance at the ledge. The shadow-figure had vanished.

Then Susannah turned away.

'Susannah!' he cried. 'Don't go!'

For an answer, Susannah scrambled through the tangled edge of the garden and plunged into the wood beyond.

'Wait!' Tom shouted. He slid down the bank and ran after her, Holly right behind him. Though Susannah did not appear to be moving particularly fast, she had already disappeared among the trees. They followed, trying to find the path she had taken; but within seconds they realized it was useless. There was no trampled undergrowth, no sounds of leaves rustling or twigs snapping ahead of them. Susannah had melted into the woodland and left no trace.

Holly leaned against a tree trunk. She was breathing heavily; not with exertion but with the aftershock of what had happened.

'Susannah saved me,' she said at last. 'She knew what was happening, and she stopped it!'

Tom nodded. 'You saw it, didn't you? The thing on the ledge.'

'Oh, yes. Oh, yes. And it . . . *called* to me. Not in words; I didn't hear a voice, or anything. I just had to go towards it.' Holly shivered. 'Nothing else mattered, and when you tried to pull me back, I'd have done anything to stop you.'

'So when Susannah called out –'

'It broke the spell somehow. The force just sort of . . . let go.'

'When the thing on the ledge appeared, what did you actually *see*?' Tom asked.

Holly pulled a face. 'I don't know. I couldn't make it out clearly; it was just a dark shape.' She frowned, trying to think back. 'You said it was like a crone, but I didn't think so. To me, it seemed more like a dwarf. A squat dwarf with a cloak and hood.'

'Straight out of a fairy story,' Tom added with a nervous laugh.

She looked soberly at him. 'Yeah. Exactly. I don't know what it is, Tom, but after what's just happened, I *do* know that it's dangerous. Susannah knows it, too. In fact I think she knows a lot about it.'

Tom agreed. 'The problem is, getting her to tell us.'

'Mmm.' Holly narrowed her eyes and peered into the wood, where it began to drop away down the valley to the creek. 'Tell me something,' she said after a few moments. 'Where did the millstream actually run?'

'I don't know exactly. It must have fed the pond up there,' he waved a hand vaguely in the direction of the bank with its boggy hollow, 'and then I suppose it ran through the millrace. According to Dad, it's been diverted or dammed or something, so it doesn't flow near the mill any more. The old bed's dried up and you can't tell where it was.'

'But the stream still exists?'

'I suppose so. Over the other side of the valley, probably, but I haven't gone looking for it.'

'Mmm,' Holly said again. 'There *is* a stream running into the creek, a bit downriver from the jetty. Is that it?'

Tom shrugged. 'Could be. Why are you so interested, anyway? I'd have thought we had more important things to worry about!'

'It wouldn't do any harm to find out, that's all. The

more we know about this place, the more chance we'll have of solving the mystery.'

'Well, I reckon we'd be better off concentrating on the Hoskin family,' said Tom. 'And that's what I'm going to do this afternoon, if Dad'll let me use his modem. Want to help?'

Holly shook her head. 'I'm going to go home. I might take a look in the parish records, to see if your mum missed anything.'

'OK.' Tom nodded agreement, then paused. 'You're all right, are you? After . . .' He jerked his head in the direction of the mill.

'Yes, I'm fine. It's funny; it almost feels now as if it happened to someone else, or didn't even happen at all. The thing on the ledge, the feeling I had, Susannah . . . it seems unreal.'

'I know what you mean,' said Tom. 'But it isn't unreal. Is it?'

Her face sobered. 'No,' she said. 'It isn't.' She hesitated, then: 'Look, I'll go now. Say thanks to your mum and dad for me; tell them I had to get back early or something.'

'What are you doing after school tomorrow?' Tom asked. 'We could get together again.'

'I don't know . . . I want a bit of time to think. I'll ring you, right? Or you ring me if you find out anything about the Hoskins, and we can decide what to do from there.'

'Fine. See you, then.'

'Yeah.' Suddenly Holly smiled. 'Say 'bye to Dublin from me, too.'

'I will.'

She walked away into the woods and vanished. Just as Susannah had done.

6

Holly didn't go directly down to the creek, where the boat was waiting. Instead, she cut across the valley and climbed the steeper slope on the far side. The trees were denser here, showering droplets on her head and reducing the daylight to a murky green in which brighter splashes dappled and danced. It was like being underwater, and she was thinking idly about that when she heard the sound of real water not far away. It was what she had been hoping for, and she followed the sound.

She couldn't see the stream until she was almost on top of it. Its bed was about two metres wide, and the water had cut a deep, fast-running channel. Tree roots protruded from the bank and hung over the water; Holly found a long stick, which she poked into the current, and judged that it was about half a metre deep. It had to be the old millstream, she thought, and it was a fair bet that it was the same one that joined the creek downstream of the jetty. All right; she knew where it went. But where did it come from?

She started to climb again, slipping and slithering and hanging on to saplings as she followed the stream against its flow. As far as she could tell she was veering away from Trevenna Mill, so if the stream had been diverted as

Tom said, it must have been sent a long way off its original course.

Then, as the trees began to thin out near the top of the valley, she saw the ruined wall ahead. It was a few metres to the right of the stream, and for the life of her Holly couldn't imagine why it had been built. It seemed to have no possible use or purpose. She scrambled up towards it – and as she got closer, she abruptly realized that the broken stonework *had* been put there for a reason. It was a double wall, and it formed a diverting channel that, once, had carried flowing water.

Holly's pulse quickened eagerly and she peered through the trees. She was nearly on a level with the mill – she could see its stone bulk beyond the wood's edge, with the grass-covered bank on the far side – and from this angle it was easy to see how the stream might once have run from the millrace to this old channel. She even thought, though she couldn't be absolutely sure, that she could see the faint line of the dried-up water course in the grass. So, then: the stream must have been diverted higher up; say, somewhere just this side of the humpbacked bridge that carried it under the village road. It had then run into the millpond and through the race, turning the wheel as it went, and these broken stones marked the place where it had been diverted again and allowed to return to its original course.

Holly straightened, gripping a low branch to stop herself slithering back down the steep valley. Well, she had made a discovery. It wasn't much use as yet but, as she had said to Tom, the more they knew, the better chance they had of learning more.

She stared at the mill again, then at the surrounding landscape, taking mental bearings so that she would be able to find the wall again. Then, carefully, she turned around and started to climb back down the valley, towards the creek and her waiting boat.

Tom spent nearly two hours on the Internet before Mr McCarthy remembered the phone bill and ordered him off. Progress had been slow and frustrating, but Tom had had one or two leads. Only the fact that he had been tempted beyond endurance to check out a few fun websites while he was at it had prevented him from following them up.

'Never mind,' his mother said when he grumbled about his father's unadventurous attitude. 'Leave me the details, and I'll carry on where you left off tomorrow.'

'But I'll be at school,' Tom protested.

'Good thing too,' said Mr McCarthy grouchily. 'Leave it to Mum; she won't waste time and get distracted.'

Defeated, Tom went to his room and made notes. There wasn't much to say: a couple of businesses in New England with the name Hoskin in them, and a Hoskins — with with an 's' — on a genealogy newsgroup, though he didn't know whereabouts in America that Hoskins lived. The chances of any of them turning up trumps was pretty remote, and Tom couldn't help feeling that he would stand a better chance with Susannah.

With that in mind, he went outside after tea and took a walk around the mill. He had a vague hope that Susannah might make herself known again, but she didn't, and eventually he climbed up the bank to the old millpond. The weather had been drier lately and the boggy area had shrunk to a small, squishy patch in the middle. The dip was very shallow, considering that it was supposed to be a pond. Dad suspected that someone had filled it in at some stage. He was thinking of digging it out again, and using the soil to build up a gentler slope from the unmade lane, to make access easier for the car.

Tom walked slowly around to the far side of the pond. It was still too wet to venture into the middle, but the ground around the edge was a bit drier underfoot than it had been. There were a lot of stones scattered about and half-buried in the earth, and he crouched down to examine one particularly large one. Its sides were quite square and even, suggesting that it had been cut or chiselled at some stage. Another stone close by looked the same, and with sudden interest Tom started to scrape away the earth between them. A third stone was revealed, joining the other two, and when he dug deeper he realized that there was at least one more layer underneath.

'Tom?' Dad's voice called from somewhere below. 'You out here?'

Tom stood up and peered over the bank, to see Dad standing by the mill. 'I'm up here,' he called back. 'And I've found something.'

'Oh?' Dad came scrambling up the bank, and Tom showed him the stones. 'They look like part of a wall,' he said.

'So they do. Hang on, I'll get a couple of spades.'

For half an hour they dug away at the stones, until a whole section of the old wall was revealed.

'You know what?' Dad said. 'I reckon this must have been where the sluice-gate used to be. You know, for letting water through to drive the wheel. The gate would have been wooden, of course, but when the mill closed down they might have filled the gateway in with stone, to make it more secure.'

'But what if the pond got too full?' Tom asked. 'The water would have to get out somewhere.' He pictured a major overflow tipping over the edge of the bank and down to the mill. It would start as a trickle, but it wouldn't take long before it became a thundering cataract . . .

'There'd have been a fail-safe of some kind,' Dad said. 'Another channel, with another gate, to feed excess water back to the stream. That gate was probably taken out altogether, but I bet we could find the channel if we looked for it. Then we'd be able to work out exactly where the millstream ran.' His eyes had an eager gleam. 'And then, if we could divert the stream again, who knows? We might get the millwheel turning one day.'

Tom had forgotten about that ambition of Dad's, and the comment gave him a sharp, unpleasant sensation in the pit of his stomach. What would happen if the wheel was made to work? What effect would it have on Susannah – or on the crooked shadow that haunted the race? Tom couldn't begin to guess, but he had a powerful feeling that it would be better to leave well alone.

He looked sidelong, uneasily, at Dad, who had started digging again. Should he say anything, try to put Dad off? He decided against it. Dad was the sort of person who, if you told him something was impossible, would be all the more determined to do it. But thankfully, Dad wasn't thinking short-term. If he ever *did* get the wheel going, it would be a long way in the future. The mystery of the haunting would be solved by then.

At least, it had better be . . .

Mr McCarthy stayed out on the bank until it was nearly dark, digging and fiddling and exploring. When he finally did come in, he had some interesting news.

'I've found the old stream bed, where it was diverted to run the mill.'

Tom and his mother both looked up from the TV, and Mrs McCarthy turned the sound down. 'Really? Where did it go? And I hope you took your wellies off *outside* the back door.'

'Of course I did. You know that scrubby patch at the

edge of our land, where it's really overgrown and all those young ash trees have come up? It came into the pond from there. Hard to find; I had to do a lot of grubbing around. But it's definitely the place.'

'What about the overflow?' Tom asked. 'Did you find that?'

'Give me a chance, I'm not Superman!' His dad grinned. 'It's a start, though. Tomorrow, I'm going to see if I can find how it was channelled back to the stream after it went through the millrace. Then we'll have a nearly complete picture.'

Lying in bed that night, Tom tried to imagine how the mill must have looked in the old days – Susannah's days – with the stream flowing down the bank, under the great wheel and then away through what was now (or would be) the garden, before going back to its original course and on down the valley. It must have been very different. Very noisy, too. The rush of the water, the rumble of the wheel, the shuddering racket of the mechanism and grinding stones . . . Impossible for anyone to sleep while the mill was operating. Or perhaps people just got used to it?

He tried to conjure up the sounds in his mind, wondering if *he* could ever have got used to it. The sound of the water came to life most vividly of all. So vividly, in fact, that he could almost . . .

Hear it . . . ?

Tom stopped breathing for a few moments, holding

the air in his lungs and keeping very still. He *could* hear water running. Not a trickle like a tap left on, but much bigger and more powerful: a full current, fast flowing.

And, crazily impossible though it seemed, it sounded as if it was only a few metres away.

He scrambled out of bed and went to the window. The moon had appeared briefly through a gap in the clouds, so the outside world showed up quite clearly in shades of grey and silver. The roof of the mill was a sharp, etched silhouette against the sky.

And he could still hear the flowing water.

Tom opened his window wide and leaned precariously out. He could see a part of the mill building, but the race and the wheel were round the other side, out of view. Was *that* where the noise was coming from? It certainly sounded like it, though he knew how easy it was for the ears to play tricks, especially in the quiet of night. A flood? No way; it was drizzling a bit, but not enough to cause that. It was something else. Something strange. And one thought was uppermost in his mind: *Susannah*.

It took moments to pull on jeans, sweatshirt and trainers. He only hoped that Dublin wouldn't hear or smell him; luck was on his side, though, and he made it to the front door without an eruption of barking from the kitchen. He had a torch, but the battery was getting low and it cast only a dim, yellowish pool of light; enough to see his way but not much use for anything else. Spare batteries were in the kitchen, though. Couldn't be helped; he'd have to make do.

At the corner of the house he paused, listening. Yes, he could hear the water, though it sounded fainter now. Peculiar: it should surely have been louder from here? Tom eased round the side of the house and padded quietly towards the mill. The water noise was still there, but it *was* faint, and sort of unreal, like something heard in a dream. He pinched himself to see if he would wake up. Nothing happened, except that it hurt. OK, then. Assuming he really was awake, he would go on and see whatever was to be seen.

The moon was to the wrong side of the mill and so the wheel and the race were in the building's black, angular shadow. Tom shone his torch but all it produced was a vague blur with no detail. Better go carefully; it would be all too easy to misjudge the distance and fall over the edge into the race. One step at a time he advanced towards the mill – then realized suddenly that the sound of the water was no longer there. The drizzle had stopped now, too, and all he could hear was the rustle of the night breeze in the trees at the wood's edge.

His brain came down to earth with a wallop, and he stood staring into the dark and calling himself every kind of idiot there was. There was no rushing water and never had been. He'd let his thoughts run away, conned himself into believing that something spooky was going on, when all it was was an overactive imagination.

Disgusted with himself, and glad that no one else had been around to see him make a fool of himself, he swung the failing torch beam in one final, almost defiant arc over the mill as he turned away.

Something moved in the faint yellow glow, and Tom stopped dead.

The torch dimmed further as the batteries gave their last gasp, and went out, leaving him in the mill's pitch black shadow. Perspiration broke out on Tom's skin and chilled, and he stared blindly into the dark.

'Who's there?' His voice was high and cracking; he forced it down a notch. 'I saw you! I know where you are!' That was a lie, but he wasn't going to admit the truth: that he had no idea where the glimpsed figure had gone, and that he was very scared.

'Come on,' he said. 'I'm not hanging around here all night – answer me!'

Nothing. Maybe the rustling breeze rose briefly, but that was all.

Tom took a step towards the mill. It was possibly a stupid thing to do, but he was trying to overcome his own fear. He tried to convince himself that the movement was just a trick played by the failing torch, that there was nothing there at all. And if that theory was wrong, and there was something there, he didn't want to turn his back on it.

Then, quite suddenly and unexpectedly, the clouds cleared and the moon came out and he saw Susannah.

She was standing on the border between deep shadow and moonlight, so that her outline was half silver and half black. Tom's mouth opened; he started to hiss her name but got no further than 'Susa—' before she jerked a finger to her lips, warning him to silence.

Then, clearly and distinctly, she whispered, 'No!'

She was running away even as Tom turned towards her, skirt flying, hair coming loose from its cap and bouncing on her shoulders. He ran after her, though he knew he couldn't catch her. Then, in the classic movie tradition, he tripped over a tussock and went sprawling on his face in the grass.

As Tom sat dizzily up, Susannah stopped and looked back. Her face was deathly pale, her eyes like smudged charcoal, and for one second Tom had a shocking insight. Susannah was frightened – no, more than that; she was *terrified*.

Behind him, in the black shadow of the mill, something uttered a cracked, metallic giggle.

Half on his feet, Tom whipped round, lost his balance and sat down hard. He started to scramble up again, and suddenly, much more loudly, Susannah called, 'Go away!'

She flapped her hands frantically, like someone trying to drive off a swarm of invisible wasps, and started to back away. But she wasn't looking at Tom. She was staring fixedly at a spot beyond him, in the deepest shadow, and the fear showed starkly in her expression.

And an ugly feeling began to creep over Tom. A feeling

of being drawn, pulled, commanded, towards the wheel and the millrace . . .

'Go!' Susannah cried again. 'Save yourself – *run!*'

Save yourself . . . The words slammed home to Tom, and though he didn't know what Susannah meant by them, instinct screamed at him to obey. He turned, lurched, nearly twisted his ankle, then got his balance back and raced for the house. He thought that Susannah was running with him, but when he snatched a wild glance to one side she wasn't there.

He reached the house, cannoned into the door frame and stopped, gasping for breath. When he looked back, all he saw was moonlight shining in an empty garden. Susannah had vanished.

Tom slid into the house, shut the door quietly and leaned against it until his heart stopped pounding and breathing was easier. Then, trying to tell himself that he wasn't ice cold and shaking all over, he padded towards the stairs and the safe haven of his room.

7

Tom couldn't concentrate at school the next day, and was thankful when lessons ended and he could go home. He was eager to see his mother and find out if she had made any progress with her search for the Hoskin family. But as he went into the house, he was surprised to hear the sound of someone playing scales on the piano.

'Mum?' He peered round the door of the small room where the piano was kept. Mrs McCarthy was there at the keyboard, with Katy in her play-pen nearby.

'Oh, hi, love.' Mum stopped playing and turned round to smile at him. 'Is it that late already?'

'What are you doing?' Tom asked.

Her smile became a grin. 'I've got some news,' she said.

'Yeah?' Tom's eyes lit up. 'About the Hoskins?'

'The – ? Oh; oh, no, not that. I haven't had time yet. No – I've got my first piano pupil!'

She went on to tell him how she had got talking to someone in the village, who knew someone else whose nine-year-old daughter wanted piano lessons, so she'd made a phone call and, 'She's coming for her first lesson after school tomorrow. I thought I'd better put in a bit of practice myself, in case I've forgotten how to teach!'

Tom tried to sound interested and pleased, but underneath he was very disappointed. He wanted to get moving on the search for the Hoskins; and after last night it seemed all the more urgent. But he hid his feelings, and only said that maybe he would have another try on the Internet later.

'Fine, if Dad says it's OK,' Mrs McCarthy agreed. 'He's gone to Penryn to see about some work, but he should be back around six.'

Tom went to his room. He had some project work to do this evening, but he couldn't concentrate on that any more than he had concentrated at school. Part of him wanted to go out to the mill and explore further, but another part wanted to stay well away from it, and he was still dithering when his mobile rang.

It was Holly. 'Hi,' she said. 'How's things? Any news?'

'Is there just!' Tom was glad to hear from her. 'Can you talk privately?'

'Sure; I'm on my mobile, in the garden. What's happened?'

'Susannah came back last night.'

'*What?*'

Tom recounted the whole eerie incident, and when he finished Holly let out a low whistle.

'That is *weird*. I wish I'd been there!'

'I wish you had, too,' said Tom with some feeling. 'I tell you, it was really creepy out there on my own!'

'Well, it's proved one thing, hasn't it?' Holly pointed

out. 'That laugh you heard – if we needed any proof that Susannah isn't the only ghost at Trevenna Mill, we've certainly got it now.

'Look,' she went on, 'I've got loads of school stuff to do in the evenings this week, and any free time I get, I want to go through those parish records. So we probably won't be able to meet up again till the weekend. But is there any way you could invite me to stay over, say, Friday night?'

'I don't see why not,' said Tom. 'We've got a spare room. The bed's a bit prehistoric, but—'

'Never mind that. I don't intend to sleep. I mean, if we're really quiet, we could set up a watch through the night and see if anything else happens.'

'Brilliant!' Tom enthused. The prospect of keeping watch alone would have scared the hell out of him, but with two it was different. 'I'll talk to Mum.'

'Catch her in a good mood, and think up a reason, so she doesn't get suspicious.'

'Will do. Oh, by the way, she hasn't got anywhere with the Internet search. But I'll see what I can track down before Friday.'

'Right,' Holly said. 'Good luck – and if anything else happens –'

'I'll be on the phone so fast, you won't know what's hit you. See you!'

Tom went back downstairs. Mum was still practising, but as he approached the piano-room a hideous thumping discord added itself to her playing, and Katy's voice rose demandingly.

'Kokky Song! Mummy sing Kokky Song!'

There was another unmusical din, then came Mum's voice, sounding long-suffering. 'All right, all right, Kitten-Kat! Leave the piano alone, and Mummy'll sing it.'

A tune began, and Mum started to sing: 'Row, row, row your boat, gently down the stream. If you see a crocodile, don't forget to—'

'*Skweeem!*' bawled Katy delightedly. 'Again! Sing it again, again, again!'

This, Tom thought, was not the ideal moment to ask a favour. He headed for the kitchen to find something to eat.

That week was a frustrating one for Tom. Everything seemed to conspire against him. School work was a pain, and left him no time for the Internet, and Mum was so busy concentrating on her piano that she seemed to have forgotten all about tracking down the Hoskins.

The only break in the cloud, so to speak, was that both his parents and the Blythes were happy for Holly to stay overnight at the mill. Tom's school was further away than Holly's, so when he got home on Friday afternoon, she had already arrived.

It had been a cloudy day with occasional short but savage showers, and Holly was accompanying Dublin on one of his forays round the wet garden. The dog saw

Tom first and came hurtling, reaching him with a flying leap and trying to lick his face off. 'Dublin, stop it! Yes, all right, hello, now get down, you dumb idiot!' He pushed the excited dog away, brushed mucky pawprints off the front of his clothes and finally had a chance to greet Holly.

'Am I glad to see you! I thought this week was never going to end.'

'Me, too.' They went indoors and as Tom dumped his school bag on the kitchen table she added, 'I managed a trawl through those old parish books, though, and I found something new. The last entry for any Hoskin was actually—'

'Did you say Hoskin?' Tom's mother came in at that moment. 'Ah! I've got something to tell you about that.'

'What?' Tom swung round eagerly.

She filled the kettle and switched it on. 'Tea, Holly? Or there's some Coke in the fridge if you prefer. Oh, yes; the Hoskins. I've found them.'

Tom and Holly both stared at her, open-mouthed, until she laughed at their expressions.

'I only said I've found the Hoskins, not won the Lottery! At least, I think I have. I got an e-mail this afternoon from a couple in Maryland, who've been reading one of the family history newsgroups. Their name isn't Hoskin, but the wife's mother's maiden name was. And *her* family emigrated from this part of Cornwall just about two hundred years ago.'

'Wow!' Tom was wide-eyed. 'That's brill, Mum! What else did they say?'

'Not much. But I've written back to them and told them a bit about our mill – not the skeleton story, of course; it might put them off – and asked if they can let me have a few more details about their ancestor.'

'That's great, Mrs McCarthy,' said Holly. 'And I've found something, too. In the parish records.' She fished in a pocket, pulled out a sheet torn from a notepad and laid it on the kitchen table. 'I'd been going through the births and deaths ones, but I suddenly thought: what about marriages? The Hoskins' children were growing up, after all. So I had a look, and I found this.'

Tom bent over the paper. Holly's writing made his look neat, but he managed to decipher it and read aloud:

' "Daniel Hoskin, of Trevenna Mill, married Mary Thomas, of Trevenna Village, in May 1817" . . . Mum, you said one of the Hoskins' children was called Samuel or Daniel, didn't you?'

'He was,' confirmed Holly. 'In fact I've got the names of all their children. Look.' Out came another piece of paper. 'The boys were Daniel, John and Peter. The girls were Ruth, Elizabeth, Jane . . . and Susannah.'

Tom grabbed the second paper and stared at it, but Mrs McCarthy was too preoccupied to notice his sharp intake of breath. 'So at least one of them married here!' she exclaimed. 'He must have been very young.'

'Eighteen,' said Holly. 'I checked in the births register. He was the eldest.'

'Well, now we're getting somewhere,' said Mrs McCarthy eagerly. 'Holly, did you look and see if Daniel and – who was it, Mary? – had any children?'

'Ah.' Holly took the paper back from Tom, who in his excitement had crumpled it in his fist. 'Yes, I did. And they didn't. But there's something weird. I had another look at the deaths register.' She smoothed the paper out. 'Mary Hoskin, née Thomas, died in 1853, and she's buried in our churchyard. But I couldn't find any mention of Daniel at all. I looked right through from the year they got married to about the 1890s. He isn't there.'

Mrs McCarthy frowned. 'That *is* strange.'

'So I went and looked for Mary's gravestone,' Holly continued. 'I found it. It just says "Sacred to the memory of Mary Grace Hoskin, departed this life twenty-fourth of November 1853, aged fifty-four years." Nothing about her being the wife of Daniel or anything, and in those days they usually put that sort of thing on the stones.'

'They did, didn't they,' Mrs McCarthy murmured. 'Curiouser and curiouser . . . So what happened to Daniel? It was a girl we found in the mill, so that possibility's out.'

Before anyone could speculate, they heard the sound of a car coming down the track. 'There's Dad,' said Mrs McCarthy. 'We'll show this to him and see what he thinks.'

Dublin rocketed out of the door so that he could be ready to leap all over Mr McCarthy as he stepped out of the car. Katy toddled after him, and Tom was sent after her to make sure she didn't fall over or off or into anything. By the time Dublin's and Katy's ritual greetings were over and they all got back inside, Holly was helping get tea ready, so it was some while before everyone had a chance to get back to the subject of the Hoskins.

Mr McCarthy was very interested by Holly's discovery, and he had an immediate theory. 'Sounds to me,' he said, 'as if, after that poor girl died, the whole family did a runner, Daniel included.'

'What, and left his young wife behind?' Mrs McCarthy was appalled.

'It's possible. If they were trying to cover her death up – which they must have been or why on earth would they have put her body in the wall? – then it would make more sense for them all to go. Maybe Daniel and what's-her-name—'

'Mary,' said Tom.

'Mary, right – maybe they weren't getting on, so he used it as a chance to run out on her, too.'

'It would explain the gravestone,' Holly agreed. 'With the name Hoskin but no mention of any husband.'

'Exactly,' said Mr McCarthy. 'Well, it's another bit of information to give the American family, isn't it?'

'Can we e-mail them tonight?' Tom asked.

'Good idea. Let Mum or me do it, though. We know how to be more tactful than you; we'll be better at finding a way to tell them that their ancestors might have been a pack of murderers who fled to America to escape the law!'

After tea, and between further rain-showers, Tom and Holly went outside to mentally map out the best vantage points for their coming night vigil.

Holly had been given a guest bedroom on the side of the house that overlooked the water wheel. That was useful but not entirely satisfactory: the wheel blocked the view of the millrace itself, and you could only see it by leaning perilously outwards and sideways.

'It'd just put the lid on it one of us fell out and brained ourselves on the ground,' Holly said as they surveyed the mill from the top of the bank where the millpond had been. 'Much safer to find somewhere out of doors, where we can get a really good view.'

Tom agreed in principle; but where? This bank was too far away; if anything happened at the race they would need a searchlight to even notice it. The obvious place to wait was by the stone piles that supported one end of the bridge. But on the whole, after his experience of the other night, Tom preferred the prospect of hanging out of a bedroom window by his heels.

'What about the mill itself?' Holly suggested when he vetoed the bridge idea. 'Where you found Susannah's bones? If we stayed near the door we could see the millwheel pretty well, but nothing would see us.'

Her casual references to bones and some*thing* seeing or not seeing them made Tom squirm inwardly, but he didn't comment. 'All right,' he said, trying to sound a lot more nonchalant than he felt. 'I suppose it's as good a place as anywhere else.'

'And you saw Susannah there, too, that first day I came,' Holly added. 'Perhaps she'll appear again.'

Tom thought for a few moments, then slowly shook his head. 'I think she only comes when there's danger of some kind,' he said. 'So if you really want me to be honest . . . I hope she doesn't show up at all tonight.'

The plan was that once everyone else in the house was asleep, they would settle themselves outside at the mill doorway and take turns to keep watch. As Tom pointed out, it was unlikely that they would both be able to stay awake all night, so if one slept while the other was on guard duty they were less likely to miss any action.

Waiting for the evening to end was frustrating. Mr McCarthy sent an e-mail to the Maryland people, wrote a few work-related letters then dozed off in front of the TV. Mrs McCarthy practised the piano, until she was defeated by piercing and persistent shouts from Katy's bedroom of 'Mumm-EEE! Want another story!' Katy flatly refused to go to sleep and was eventually brought downstairs, where she pulled Dublin's tail, sang at the top of her voice until she woke Mr McCarthy up, and generally made a thorough nuisance of herself. Tom could cheerfully have strangled her, but Holly said, 'If you can't beat 'em, join 'em,' and played horsey on all fours with the little girl until Katy finally ran out of steam.

'It's obvious you haven't got a kid brother or sister,' Tom said sourly as his mother bore Katy away back to bed. 'If you had, you wouldn't be so keen to indulge Katy!'

'She's a sweetheart, really,' Holly said. 'Anyway, I had an ulterior motive. The sooner I could wear her out, the sooner your mum and dad can finish whatever they want to do and get to bed.'

She had a point. Mr McCarthy was yawning hugely now and muttering about making hot chocolate, and when Mrs McCarthy came back downstairs she firmly shut the piano lid and turned off the light in the room where it was kept.

'About time you two were asleep,' she said to Tom and Holly. 'Holly, I'd grab the bathroom while you can, if I were you. Tom's usually in there for about a week.'

'Right, I will. Thanks, Mrs McCarthy.' Holly flicked Tom a significant glance. 'Goodnight, everyone.'

Nearly another hour had passed before everyone in the house was finally in bed. Tom, sitting in his room with the light off, strained his ears for any more tell-tale sounds, and at last, deciding that his parents must surely be asleep by now, tiptoed out of the door.

He met Holly on the landing. She had her jacket on over her clothes and was carrying her shoes in one hand. She followed him back to his room, where she whispered, 'You've been ages – I thought you'd gone to sleep!'

'Shh! I wanted to be sure about Mum and Dad, that's all. Got your torch?'

'Yep. Put new batteries in yours?'

'Of course I have! Right; come on, then.'

They crept down the stairs and past the kitchen door, letting out their breaths and uncrossing their fingers when Dublin didn't bark. The sky was beginning to clear but the moon wasn't up yet, so they made their way in near-total darkness to the mill. Tom's nerves were jangling by the time they reached it, but Holly seemed totally calm. He envied her. But then, she hadn't been here last time.

'Shall I take first watch?' she suggested. 'I couldn't sleep anyway.'

'Neither could I. But OK; if you want. I'll make myself comfortable . . .' He looked dubiously at the stone and earth floor, '. . . Well, I'll try. At least the ground's dry here, I suppose. Two hours?'

'Let's make it an hour and a half. That gives us two watches each before anyone else is likely to be getting up.'

She sat down by the gaping doorway as Tom settled as best he could on the floor. For all his nerves, he suspected that this was going to be boring. He wished he had brought a book; but then he would have needed torchlight to read it and that would only have flattened the batteries all over again.

'Do you want to talk?' he asked after a few minutes of silence.

'No,' said Holly. 'I might miss something. Shut up.'

Tom closed his eyes and shut up.

Nothing happened during Holly's first vigil. Tom dozed off once or twice, but it was a broken, uneasy sleep, filled with peculiar half-dreams that he was glad to shake off. At last Holly got up and came over to him.

'Your turn,' she said. 'Wake me at about three.'

'Right.' Tom heaved himself stiffly to his feet. He yawned as he reached the door. Typical: he was tired now. Oh, what the heck. It was only an hour and a half. He could manage that easily.

He sat down with his back against the door opening, and tried to think of something to pass the time.

Tom didn't think of anything to pass the time. In fact, he told himself after a while, this was probably going to be the dullest hour and a half he had ever spent in his life. There was nothing to look at, nothing to do, he was uncomfortable, and getting progressively colder from lack of movement.

Holly had fallen asleep about five minutes after he took over the watch. The moon had risen now; it was almost full and by its light he could dimly see her humped shape curled up on the floor. She snored slightly, which made him smile. He'd tell her about that later.

At least an hour must have passed by now. Shielding his torch with latticed fingers, Tom looked at his watch. Twenty minutes gone. Oh, *great*. This was so *tedious*. He felt sleepy. *Go on*, he told himself. *Shut your eyes. Just for a few moments. It won't do any harm.*

He woke with a start, as if something had disturbed him, and for several seconds he had no idea where he was. When he did realize, he shifted his position and winced as stiff, chilled muscles twinged.

What time was it? He looked at his watch again and to his dismay saw that it was three-thirty. He'd slept through his watch and way over – Holly would be livid! Moving awkwardly because of the stiffness, Tom got up and turned to the building's interior.

'Holly.' He groped to where she ought to be and felt for a shoulder to shake. 'Holly, wake up!'

She didn't answer, and he flicked his torch on.

Holly's coat lay folded on the ground; he could see the indentation of her head where she had used it as a pillow. But Holly wasn't there.

Tom's stomach gave a queasy lurch. He took a grip on himself and tried to be rational. Maybe she had needed a pee or something, and had gone back to the house or even to a handy bush. She would be back in a minute. So he waited. But Holly didn't return. Was she playing a trick on him? Had she woken up, seen him sleeping, and hidden to scare him and teach him a lesson?

'Holly!' He stepped outside and hissed her name, shining the torch around. 'OK, I admit it, I screwed up! I'm sorry. Get back at me some other way tomorrow, but let's call it quits for now, all right?'

Nothing. No voice, no movement in the torch beam. The queasy feeling came back and Tom started to swing the torch around, quartering the ground for clues, footprints, anything. He drew a complete blank, and was about to turn the torch off to conserve it when a small, distant noise made him freeze.

He told himself he was wrong. He told himself he had imagined it. But truly, he knew it was real. Because he had heard that same sound once before.

From the direction of the millrace, it was a high, cracked giggle of laughter.

8

The moon had vanished behind a cloud, and Tom didn't dare switch his torch on. He had moved, sneakingly, furtively, along the mill wall until he was as close to the wheel and the race as he had the courage to go, but he couldn't see a thing in the dark. Holly could be anywhere. And as for whatever had uttered that diabolical giggle . . .

He fought a powerful urge to run away, round the mill and into the house where he would be safe. It was still possible that Holly was teasing him, or had gone for a pee, or any one of a dozen other and increasingly unlikely ideas that his mind had managed to come up with. But in his heart he knew that none of those ideas was true.

Then abruptly the moon came out again, and he saw her.

His heart nearly stopped altogether. Holly was at the top of the stone piles that supported one end of the mill race bridge. She was silhouetted clearly against the moon-brightened sky, and she was gripping the bridge's rail. Even as Tom watched, she slid one foot forward, on to the first of the rotting planks.

Tom wanted to scream a warning to her, but he was too frightened. Something was lurking there in the dark, and if he shouted, it would hear him. He didn't want that; it was chicken, it was cowardly, but he didn't want it. Instead he lurched forward and started to run, covering the ground between himself and the bank like a scuttling rabbit. Holly was unaware of him. Both her feet were on the bridge now; she swayed slightly as if she couldn't quite get her balance. Then she took another step.

'Holly!' From the base of the wall Tom hissed as loudly as he dared. She didn't hear, or she chose to ignore him.

Or perhaps she didn't have a choice . . .

Stuffing the torch in a jacket pocket, Tom started to climb up the stonework. He slipped back several times in his hurry, scraping palms and wrists, but at last he made it to the top and stood upright. Holly was more than a metre on to the bridge by this time; he made to start after her then stopped as he realised how risky that could be. The bridge was so decayed; there was a chance it might take Holly's weight, but not his as well.

'*Holly!*' he called more loudly. Still Holly didn't respond – but in the dank moon-shadow on the far side of the race, it seemed to him that something moved sluggishly.

His heart beating so hard that it hurt, Tom gripped the bridge rails with one hand and leaned out as far as he could. His other hand groped in a straining effort – if he could just touch her, physically, it might break the spell –

He couldn't reach her. One step on to the bridge and he might just do it. But if he took that step, the bridge could give way. His stomach roiled at the thought of the drop to the bottom of the dried-out race. If they were lucky, they would only break their backs . . .

'Holly! Holly, listen to me!' It was a last-ditch attempt and he knew it was hopeless. Holly was completely oblivious; whatever spell the thing by the wheel had cast, it was too strong for either of them to break. Tom had no other choice; he had to follow her on to the bridge, drag her back by force and pray that the planks held.

He drew breath to make the first nerve-racking move –

And from below him a voice called, 'No! You mustn't, you mustn't!'

Tom started violently, looked down – and saw Susannah. She was at the foot of the stone supports, pallid and grey in the moonlight, staring up at him with wide, frightened eyes. As their gazes met he expected her to flee as she had done before. But instead, she began to babble at him, a distraught flood of words accompanied by flapping and wringing of her hands. Her agitation, and her strong Cornish accent, made it impossible for Tom to understand most of what she was saying, but he made out, 'can't keep it away from you' – 'I am not strong enough' – 'too afraid of it'. She was obviously terrified; yet it seemed she desperately wanted to help them. *Too afraid. Can't keep it away . . .*

'Susannah, you've got to do something!' Tom pleaded. 'Go to Holly, get her off the bridge!'

Susannah shook her head and covered her face with both hands. 'I can't!' she moaned. 'I'm too weak, I have no courage! Oh, dear God, help us all!'

Holly, taking one slow step at a time, was nearly halfway across the bridge. On the edge of his vision Tom saw the sluggish, shadowy movement again, and it snapped his mind suddenly into focus. Time was running out. Susannah couldn't – or wouldn't – do anything; Holly's sole hope lay in his own hands. And he could think of only one thing to do.

He snatched the torch from his pocket, lined it up so that it was pointing directly at the millwheel, and switched it on.

The white beam lit up the wheel like a theatre spotlight, and he heard a girl scream. He didn't know whether it was Holly or Susannah, and at that moment he didn't care. All his attention was fixed, in horror and disbelief, on what the torchlight had revealed.

It was crouching on the ledge, and the beam had caught it full on. A shapeless bundle of rags (though they weren't rags; they were something else, unnameable) from the midst of which a distorted face stared back at him. Images slammed into Tom's mind: white skin with an awful greenish sheen to it; a slack, wet mouth working soundlessly; staring, expressionless eyes like the eyes of a dead fish . . . He felt bile coming up into his throat and he gagged, lurching sideways, swinging the torch away from the monstrosity. The torch beam danced wildly as a shrill, whistling sound like a thin wail of anger reached him from across the race; there was a flurrying and scrabbling – then total silence.

Tom found himself leaning over the bridge rail with the torch shining uselessly on the grass below. Susannah had vanished; there was a burning, metallic taste in his mouth and he thought he must have thrown up, though he couldn't remember doing it. His mind was reeling; every nerve felt as if an electric current were going through it –

'Tom . . .'

The voice shook with fright, and came from the bridge. *Holly* . . . Tom forced himself upright and raised the torch. Holly was standing motionless on the bridge, gripping the rails as though they were a lifeline. She had tried to turn round but had only managed to make it halfway before her courage failed.

'Tom . . .' she wavered. 'How did I . . .'

'Don't ask!' Tom interrupted sharply, not wanting to give her any chance to think about it until she was safely back on solid ground. 'Don't be scared. You're only a couple of metres out, and the bridge'll hold your weight. Come back slowly . . . that's it, one foot . . . now the other . . .' He shifted the torch so that it shone on the end of the bridge, giving her a goal. 'Don't look down, just look at the light. See how close it is. That's the way . .'

Slowly and unsteadily, Holly made it to safety. She grabbed Tom and hugged him as she came off the bridge, and he thought that she was crying.

'Come on.' He squeezed her, hard. 'Let's get off this bank.'

She sniffed and let him help her down the stone piling to level ground. Then, with real feeling, she said a word that would have horrified the Reverend Blythe. Tom smiled thinly, knowing that it was her way of dealing with the shock and bringing herself back to something like normal.

He said, 'OK now?'

'Yes.' She nodded. 'Sure. Tom, I—'

'Look, before you say anything, I want to. I screwed up. I fell asleep when I was supposed to be watching, and because of that, you nearly – well, you know. I'm sorry. I really am. You've got every right to be livid with me.'

Holly sniffed again and wiped her eyes impatiently on her sleeve. 'I'm not livid with you,' she said. 'And I'll tell you why. I reckon if you'd been awake too, you'd have been caught the same way as I was. Then there'd have been nobody to help either of us.'

Tom's eyes narrowed. 'Do you remember what happened?' he asked.

'Oh, yes.' Holly's face and voice were grim. 'On the bridge, when the spell broke, I was completely confused for a minute. But I remember it all now.' She looked nervously over her shoulder at the wheel, invisible in the dark. 'Can we go back to the building? I don't feel too good about staying out here.'

112

She kept a hold of Tom's hand as they hurried back into the mill, and only relaxed when they were through the door and under cover. Then she sank down on her folded coat, let go a long breath, and started her story.

'I woke up and I could hear this sound,' she said. 'It was coming from somewhere near the millwheel, and it was weird, like water running but not quite. Then I saw that you'd gone to sleep. I was really cross with you; I was about to wake you up, but . . . this feeling started *tugging* at me, telling me to leave you alone and come and look by myself.' Another sniff. 'I fell for it like a complete prat. I thought: serve Tom right if I solve the whole mystery and he misses out. I must have been out of my *mind*.'

'You weren't,' said Tom. 'You were hypnotized.'

'Yeah; or ensnared, or enspelled, or whatever the technical term is. So I went. As soon as I got near the wheel I just *knew* there was something there. I was going to switch my torch on – you know, shine a light, boldly challenge it, all the big, brave rubbish. But I couldn't. Something stopped me. And then . . . then I found myself going towards the bridge, and though I knew it was dangerous, I couldn't make myself stop.'

'That happened to you once before, didn't it?' said Tom. 'Remember? The first time you came, you felt this compulsion to go over the bridge.'

'Yes, I did, didn't I? And that was in broad daylight.' Holly shivered. 'This was worse, though. Much stronger.

113

And I couldn't see anything; I didn't know what was waiting for me on the other side.' She looked slantwise at him. 'Did you shout at me?'

'Yes. Several times.'

'I didn't hear a thing. I had no idea you were even there, till you switched your torch on and I saw that . . . that . . .'

'Don't even think about what we saw. It made me throw up.'

She nodded. 'I don't know why it wanted me to go to it, or what it would've done when I got there. I just knew that I had to go. I was scared, I was *terrified*, but I had to go!'

'All right, all right,' Tom said soothingly as she started to shake. 'Don't tell me any more now, OK? I want to tell *you* something. Susannah was there.'

'What?' Holly looked at him in amazement. 'Where? When?'

'At the bridge.' Tom described how Susannah had appeared and begged him not to go after Holly, and what he had been able to decipher from her babbling.

'She knows what that thing is,' he said. 'I'm certain she does. And she's as frightened of it as we are – more, maybe, or she'd have tried to help.'

'Where did she go?' Holly's gaze shifted around as if she half expected Susannah to step out of the solid wall.

'I don't know. I was more worried about you than her.'

'We've got to find her, Tom! She keeps trying to warn us about danger, but how the hell can we avoid it if we don't know how? We need Susannah's help. We've *got* to persuade her to talk to us!'

Tom saw the sense in that, and made a decision. 'All right,' he said. 'We've tried asking, and that hasn't got us very far. So maybe it's time to start demanding.'

He got up and went to the doorway, looking out over the silvered garden.

'Susannah,' he said sternly. 'I think you're somewhere near, and you can hear me. So listen. We've had enough of your games, and we want them to stop. Oh, sure, it's easy turning up after everything's gone wrong, saying "told you so" and vanishing again before we can do anything. *Really* helpful! But we don't know what we're up against, and you're the only person who can tell us. So play fair, before somebody gets *killed*!'

Tom was privately quite pleased with his speech, but when a minute or so had passed and nothing happened, his spirits sagged.

'Well, it was worth a try,' he said disconsolately, dragging his feet back to where Holly sat.

Holly nodded sympathetically. 'Maybe she's just not the halfway decent person we thought she was. Maybe she doesn't actually care.'

From the darker shadows in the depth of the mill, a voice said,' 'Tisn't that I don't care! But I was afraid . . .'

Shock slammed through them both and they whipped

round, to see Susannah standing two metres away.

Holly made an inarticulate noise – it was, after all, the very first time she had seen the ghost for herself. Tom was more self-controlled.

'Hello, Susannah,' he said. 'You came back, then.'

Susannah lowered her gaze and for a moment her outline wavered a little. 'Yes,' she said. 'I heard you, and I was ashamed.'

Holly was recovering herself now, and spoke up. 'Are you really . . .' Her voice squeaked; she tried again. 'Are you really a . . . ghost?'

Susannah turned to look sadly at her. 'I b'lieve in truth I must be, miss. I died, see, but I did not go to rest in Heaven, as it promises in the Bible. I stayed here. I *must* stay here.'

Holly swallowed. 'The burial service . . . your funeral . . . We thought it would set you free . . .'

'I know. It was a kindly deed and I thank you with all my heart. It was a great comfort to have the proper prayers said for me. But I must stay here.'

'Why?' Tom asked.

She looked away again. 'Because I must.'

Holly gave Tom a glance that said, *She isn't going to tell us. Don't push her.* 'Susannah,' she asked gently, 'did you live here at the mill?'

'Oh, yes.' Susannah gazed around and smiled, as if she was seeing into a happier past that was invisible to Tom and Holly. 'With Father and Mother, and Ruth and

Daniel and all the younger ones . . . Daniel wed Mary when I was fourteen, and they took a cottage in the village. But the others all stayed, until . . .' She frowned, and her tone changed. 'No. I mustn't speak of it.'

Must and *mustn't*, Tom thought. Why? What was preventing Susannah from speaking freely? He licked his lips and decided to take the risk of jumping in with a blunt question.

'Susannah,' he said, 'how did you die?'

Holly protested, '*Tom*!' but she was too late. Susannah's face turned pinched and hollow; quickly she turned away, and her figure started to fade.

'Susannah, wait!' If looks could have killed, the one Holly shot Tom would have vaporized him on the spot. But Susannah hesitated.

'Please don't go.' Holly spoke very softly. 'Tom didn't mean to upset you. But he's a boy, and boys never think before they open their mouths!'

'Coming from you—' Tom hissed.

'*Shut up, Tom*! Susannah . . . Please?'

Susannah's spectral figure shimmered, shivered . . . and stabilized again. 'I will stay,' she said harshly. 'It is right that Tom should ask his question. It is right that he should want to know the truth, and I . . . I want to tell him. But I am so afraid . . .'

'Of *it*?' Tom probed, more gently.

She nodded, and Holly said, 'Is there some way we can help you overcome your fear?'

A shake of the head this time, then Susannah hesitated and said, 'Sometimes its strength is less . . . When the moon is weak, and there has been no rain; then it does not come. I think perhaps it cannot.' She turned and looked at them – an intense, pleading look. 'I will tell you then. In daylight, if the – the moon is right and the weather dry. I will tell you then.'

'She means at new moon,' Holly whispered to Tom. 'It's nearly full now – new moon's two weeks away!'

'It must be then!' Susannah had heard her. 'Or I can't. I *dare* not!'

'All right,' said Holly. 'Then we'll just have to wait. And pray for dry weather.'

'And in daylight,' Susannah repeated. 'It must be in daylight!'

'She doesn't want much, does she?' Tom muttered.

'Shut up!' Holly elbowed him in the ribs. 'We agree, Susannah. But will you come then?'

The ghost looked blank. 'Oh, yes. If you give your word, 'tisn't right to break it.'

Holly nodded. 'We can trust her,' she said to Tom.

'I hope so.' Tom was less convinced, and frowned at Susannah. 'How are we going to find you when it's the right time?'

'Call me,' said Susannah. 'I will come. I'm always here.'

It was the best they could hope for, and they both knew it. Susannah continued to watch them for a few moments more, then she said, 'I will go now.' She paused again. 'Tom . . . have you the flower still?'

Tom felt a pang. 'Yes. I pressed it.'

'Keep it for me.' She smiled, a sweet, sad smile. Then she stepped into the deep shadow and was gone.

For a long time neither Tom nor Holly spoke. Then at last Holly broke the silence.

'She's hardly any older than us . . .'

Tom glanced sideways at her, and even in the dimness he saw a wet gleam on her cheeks. He was on the verge of crying himself, and to stop it he switched the torch on and looked at his watch.

'It's nearly five o'clock,' he said, angry that his voice had a quaver in it. 'Be getting light soon. We'd better go back to the house.'

Holly sniffed. 'Yeah.'

'Come on.' He reached out and gave her arm a little shake. 'We've both had enough for one night.'

She didn't answer but stood up, slipping her coat on and hugging it tightly around herself. They left the mill quietly. At the door Holly looked back.

'Goodnight, Susannah,' she said. Then she followed Tom out into the silent garden.

9

Tom and Holly were both very subdued the next morning. Tom couldn't stop yawning – hardly surprising after so little sleep – and Holly was pale and preoccupied. As soon as breakfast was over she said she ought to be going home, thanked Mr and Mrs McCarthy very politely for letting her stay the night, and collected her coat from the hall.

'I'll come part of the way with you,' Tom said quickly. 'I can give Dublin his morning walk at the same time.' He badly wanted a chance to talk to her and was dismayed that she seemed so eager to get away. Holly nodded but didn't say anything, and they left the house with Dublin pulling joyfully on his lead.

Holly set off towards the valley path, giving the mill building a wide berth. She had her hands thrust deep in her pockets and was looking resolutely at the ground ahead of her, a frown on her face. Hauling the dog back to something like a walking pace, Tom said, 'Why are you in such a hurry to go? We need to talk!'

'I know,' said Holly. 'But I can't; not yet. I want some time to think before I say anything.'

'You're not going to bottle out on me, are you?'

She flashed him an angry glance. 'No! After what

happened, it's even more important that we get to the bottom of this! But last night . . . well, it shook me up. I'd never come face to face with Susannah before; and as for the other thing . . .' She hunched her shoulders as if protecting herself against some invisible threat. 'Before, it all seemed quite fun, and not very real. Now, though, it's got a lot more serious.'

'You're scared?'

'Of course I am! And don't try to tell me you're not, because—

'All right, all right! I am, and I never said I wasn't, so don't blow a fuse!'

She looked at him again, for longer this time. 'Sorry . . . I'm all strung out this morning; I didn't mean . . . Oh, look, I might as well tell you. When we got back to bed last night, I didn't go to sleep. I couldn't. I kept thinking about what we saw when you shone your torch on the millwheel. I couldn't get it out of my head.' She stopped and pulled one hand out of her pocket, clutching something. 'So I tried to draw it.'

She held out a sheet of paper, which she had rolled into a long cigar and then folded in half. Tom took it but didn't unfold it.

'Go on,' she said. 'Look at it, and tell me if it's anything like what you saw.'

She took Dublin's lead from him, and slowly he did as she asked. There were several sketches on the paper, hastily done in ballpoint, and a cold sensation ran the length of Tom's spine as he looked at them. They were just impressions. But the hunched, ragged outline, the shapeless mouth, the dead-fish eyes – Holly had captured that brief, shocking glimpse, as he remembered it, all too well.

He folded the paper again, fast, not wanting to look any more. 'Yeah,' he said in a tight, strained voice. 'That's about it.'

Holly put the paper back in her pocket. 'Well,' she said, 'at least we both saw the same thing. I was starting to think I'd hallucinated.'

'What do you think it is . . . ?'

'God knows. Or maybe not; maybe even God couldn't come up with an answer. I'd have to ask my dad . . .' She tried to laugh at the attempted joke, but it didn't work and she gave up. 'Come on,' she said, 'let's walk on.'

She held on to Dublin's lead, as if controlling the dog helped to keep her thoughts on solid ground. After a minute or so she said, 'We're going to have to wait, aren't we? After what Susannah said. She won't tell us anything until the conditions she talked about are right.'

'New moon and dry weather.' Tom looked around at the trees, which were still dripping from yesterday's showers. 'Some hope! Is there ever a day when it doesn't rain in Cornwall?'

Holly gave a harsh little laugh. 'Don't you know the joke? A tourist asks a kid that question, and the kid says, "How would I know? I'm only seven."'

'Ha, ha. Seriously, though, if it belts down all over the new moon time, then what do we do?'

'Wait till the next one, or the next.' Dublin charged into a bush, nearly pulling her with him. 'Heel, Dublin!'

'He doesn't know "heel" yet. Or if he does, he doesn't take any notice. Look, Holly, can we *afford* to wait? It's all very well for Susannah to insist that everything has to be right, but last night was no joke! What if it happened to one of us again? Or,' as an even worse thought occurred to him, 'to someone else? It could be Katy next time!'

'Believe me, I've thought about that,' said Holly grimly. 'But how can we force Susannah? We've just got to go along with what she says. We haven't got any choice.'

Tom couldn't argue with that, and, sobered, neither of them spoke again until they emerged from the wood on to the foreshore. Holly had walked from the village yesterday rather than bring the boat. Now she looked at the creek's grey-green water lapping at the shale and weed at the shore's edge.

'Tide's coming in,' she said. 'I'd better get a move on, or I'll have to wade the last bit.'

'But—' Tom began helplessly.

She looked hard at him. ' "But" nothing. We're stuck with it, and that's that. Just watch out for yourself, and keep an eye on your kid sister. And if anything else happens, ring me.'

'OK,' he agreed, defeated. Holly handed over Dublin's lead. Then as she was about to go, she said, 'Oh, there's one thing you could do. See if you can work out *exactly* where the millstream used to run, when it was diverted to work the wheel.'

'Why?' he asked.

'It's just a hunch, and I haven't got any real reason for it. But I think it might be important. See you, then. And . . . take care, yeah?'

'Yeah.' He watched her hurry away along the shore, and wished he didn't feel so afraid.

Tom was on edge all the next week. For one thing there was the weather to worry about, because every time it looked like clearing into a halfway decent dry spell, the respite only lasted a short time before the rain came back again. Secondly, there was the constant lurking fear that something terrible was going to happen. He wished he hadn't had the ugly thought about Katy, and each day he got home from school as fast as he could, to make sure she was all right. He was frightened for his parents, too, though he reasoned that, being adult and 'sensible', they were a lot less likely to run into trouble. Once people got older and stopped believing in the supernatural, the supernatural seemed to lose its power over them. Tom would have given a lot not to believe in the thing in the millrace. But that was a complete impossibility.

He only heard from Holly once, a quick call on his mobile to say hi and was he all right, and to remind him about checking out the stream. Though he didn't admit it to her, Tom was not at all keen on doing that; at least, not physically. However, he had started looking in the school library for anything on local history. He hadn't come up with much so far, but at least he felt he was trying.

He and Holly did not get together over the weekend. It was wet anyway, which was worrying, and they agreed that it would be better not to do anything that might provoke trouble until they had had their promised meeting with Susannah. Nothing strange happened at the mill, and Tom did his best to distract himself by repainting the walls of his bedroom. He had managed to hide most of the ghastly pea-green with posters, but more than enough still showed. By Sunday afternoon three walls were bright yellow and the fourth wall a kind of purplish-red. Katy announced, 'Custard!' when she saw it, and Dad said it looked worse than the pea-green but if Tom had no taste who was he to argue. Tom put his posters back, went to sleep with the smell of new paint in his nostrils, and felt relieved that the weekend had gone by without anything going wrong.

Then on Monday, as the McCarthys were finishing tea, the phone rang.

'I'll get it,' said Mrs McCarthy. 'It's probably Sally's mother, about tomorrow's piano lesson. You two can start clearing the table.'

She went into the sitting-room. Tom and his father didn't hear her surprised exclamation, and didn't bother to cock an ear to what was said afterwards. But when five minutes or so later she came back, her face was a picture of excitement.

'You'll never guess who that was!' she exclaimed.

Tom made an I'd-better-be-polite-but-I'm-not-really-interested noise and Mr McCarthy said, 'Genghis Khan? Queen Victoria? Martian invaders?'

She gave him a withering look. 'Don't be an idiot. It was Jane Redmay.'

Tom and his father stared blankly. 'Who?' said Tom.

'Jane Redmay! Oh, you two really are *dumb* . . . From Maryland? The Hoskin descendant? All the e-mails?'

The connection clicked and Tom's eyes widened. 'Mum! You mean—'

'I mean, she's just called from the States, and her ancestors *were* the same Hoskins, and . . .' Mrs McCarthy paused for dramatic emphasis: 'The family's coming to England for a holiday, and they're going to visit us!'

'Cool!' said Tom. 'When?'

'Well, they're flying over pretty soon, but they haven't sorted their schedule out yet. Jane will let me know. And in the meantime she's e-mailing some family history details, and anything we know, could we send to her in return, so they've got lots of info before they arrive.'

'Ah,' said Tom's dad. 'Have you told her about the you-know-what yet?' He didn't use the word 'skeleton' because Katy was in the room.

'Well, no,' Mrs McCarthy admitted. 'I'm not quite sure how to break it to them.'

'Gently, I'd say. It fact it might be better not to say anything about it until they get here.'

'Possibly . . . I'll have to give it some thought.'

'Can I ring Holly and tell her, Mum?' Tom asked.

'Yes, if you want to. Oh, I can tell Jane what Holly discovered in the parish records, can't I? About Daniel Hoskin and Mary Thomas, and the inscription on Mary's grave. She might be able to shed some light on it. Thanks for reminding me, Tom.'

Tom took his mobile to his bedroom, with Katy puffing up the stairs after him on all fours. Holly answered almost immediately, and he told her the news.

'Whoo!' she said when he finished. 'They must be keen!'

'They were coming over to England anyway, Mum said. But yeah, they're certainly not ones for hanging about.'

'There's only one thing that worries me,' Holly said. 'How's Susannah going to react? I mean, they're her relatives, aren't they? If they ran out after she died, what will she feel about them now?'

That hadn't occurred to Tom. 'It *was* two hundred years ago,' he reasoned, though a little uneasily. 'They're totally different people; they're not even called Hoskin any more.'

'I know. But it could cause problems. And we can hardly explain to them.'

Tom considered. 'Maybe we shouldn't tell Susannah about them.'

'She'll find out for herself when they show up, won't she? For all we know, she could be well aware of it already; she might have heard you all talking about it.'

He looked quickly over his shoulder, alarmed by the idea that Susannah could be invisibly listening and watching. There was no sign of her, of course, and he said, 'I think we should tell her. Like you said, she'll find out eventually, and if she knows we've been keeping it from her she won't ever trust us again.'

'Good point. OK; then we'd better do it when we meet her. New moon's on Thursday; I looked it up. So start praying for a dry weekend!'

'Right,' said Tom. 'And if anything else happens about the Americans, I'll call you.'

He hung up. Katy by this time had plonked herself on the floor and was looking at the pictures in a sci-fi magazine she had pulled down from the table along with two school books and a box of computer discs.

'Kitten-Kat, look what you've done!' Tom started to gather the scattered discs. '*Mustn't* touch Tom-Tom's things! Naughty!'

Katy ignored the telling-off and stabbed a finger at the magazine. It was a still from a movie: alien-looking buildings against an alien-looking sky, with some sort of laser war going on. With an angelic smile Katy said, 'Sklington.'

'What?' said Tom. Something crawled under his skin. 'Don't be silly, there aren't any skling— skeletons in the picture. Lasers, look. Big lights. Pretty.'

'Not lights,' Katy declared firmly. 'Sklington.'

He snatched up the magazine and put it out of her reach. She stared at him, frowning, and for a moment it looked as if she might start to howl. But then the frown cleared and she clambered clumsily to her feet.

'*Nasty* sklington,' she said. 'Don't want to play with it. Find Dubly.'

She toddled out of the door and Tom heard her going slowly downstairs.

He wished that she hadn't said what she did.

On Wednesday the weather cleared up. Tom could hardly believe the good luck, and was certain that it couldn't possibly last. But it did, and on Friday evening the weather forecaster said confidently that they were in for at least a week of sunny weather.

And Tom's luck did not stop there. Mum said that, as it looked as if it was going to be nice, she and Dad were going to have a day off tomorrow and take a drive out to see some scenery. Did Tom want to come?

'Er . . . no, thanks,' said Tom, crossing his fingers that his parents wouldn't insist. 'I've got school work and stuff – and I sort of arranged to see Holly.'

'Oh, right,' Mrs McCarthy said. 'Do you want to invite Holly over here? If you do, I'll leave you a couple of pizzas.'

'Thanks, Mum, that'd be great.' He paused. 'You're taking Katy, aren't you?'

She grinned. 'Don't worry, you won't have to spend your Saturday babysitting! We'll show her some of the beaches. She'll love that.'

So, Mum, Dad *and* Katy would all be out of the way. *Someone up there must like me*, Tom thought, and went to ring Holly and tell her the good news.

His parents and Katy left after breakfast the next morning, and Holly was at the mill by half-past ten.

'Well, if Susannah's conditions aren't right today, they never will be,' she said, squinting at the brilliant sky. 'We couldn't have asked for anything better.'

'Let's just hope she keeps her promise,' said Tom.

'Oh, I think she will. Remember what she said about it being wrong to break your word? People thought like that much more in those days, and they were more religious, too. She'll answer us.'

They made sure that Dublin was shut in the house, and went to the end of the garden where the wood began. It seemed logical that Susannah would feel happier outside than in the mill building, so much closer to the source of danger. All the same, Tom still had some doubts as he spoke her name into thin air and asked her to appear. What if she did break her promise? What if she was simply too frightened to help them? What if—

In the house, Dublin barked loudly, once. A patch of

sunlight between two trees distorted briefly, and Susannah was there.

Tom was shocked, not just by the suddenness of her arrival, but by her appearance, too. He had only had the briefest glimpses of her in daylight before, and was now completely thrown by how *real* she looked. She seemed as solid and alive as himself and Holly. Only her old-fashioned clothes struck a wrong note. But then he saw that there were oddities. Her skin had almost no colour at all and, more disturbingly, if he looked very carefully he thought he could make out the faint green haze of the trees through her body. It was disconcerting and he turned his head quickly away.

Holly, too, was staring, and quite possibly thinking the same things as Tom. But she showed no sign of it as she said, 'Hello, Susannah. Thank you for answering us.'

'I gave my word.'

'And we've kept ours,' said Tom. 'It's daylight, new moon, and there hasn't been any rain for a few days.'

'Yes.' Susannah looked down and pushed at a tussock of grass with one buckled shoe. The grass blades didn't move. 'So now I must tell you what happened to me . . .'

'That's what we want,' said Holly quietly. 'Please.'

The ghost nodded. 'Come, then. I'll show you.'

She moved away. Tom was never sure whether she walked or glided; whenever he tried to tell, her feet seemed to blur so that he couldn't quite see them. He and Holly didn't speak as she led them back through the garden and past the house. Dublin barked again as they went by, and Susannah hesitated.

'It's all right,' said Tom. 'It's only my dog, and he's shut in.'

She smiled at him over her shoulder. 'I know. And I'm not afraid. I like dogs. We always had dogs, before . . .' Her expression changed and abruptly she walked on.

Surprisingly, she led them up the bank to the drained-out millpond with its reedy edges, from where they looked down on the mill and the race.

' 'Twas all that different when we lived here,' she said. 'The millstream ran into the pond, then the sluice-gates let the water through, and that drove the wheel.'

Tom said eagerly, 'We found where they used to be! There's a wall there now, but Dad said there would have been wooden gates when the mill was working. And he said something about a fail-safe . . .' Susannah looked blank, and he fished for a word she would understand. 'An overflow? In case the pond got too full?'

'Oh, yes. 'Twas there,' she said, pointing. 'But there's no need of it now. The stream was let back to its old course, see, so . . .' Suddenly a peculiar, almost agonized expression crossed her face. 'That was what went wrong! When they let the stream go they should have sent it on its way, they should have made *sure* – but they didn't know, and they wouldn't have believed . . .' Her voice was rising sharply but with a sudden effort she checked herself. 'I'm . . . sorry. Forgive me.'

'You said, "they should have sent it on its way",' Holly prompted gently. 'What do you mean? Is it . . . something to do with the water?'

Susannah nodded. 'I have been trying to think of the right way to tell you my story, but I don't b'lieve I have the words; and if I had, I – I don't b'lieve I would have the courage to say them. So I think I must show you. I think 'tis the only way to make you understand.'

Tom and Holly exchanged a glance. 'What do you mean, show us?' Tom asked uncertainly.

Susannah stared down at the mill with a strange, blind stare. 'I mean, to make you see what did happen . . . the way it did happen. As if you were there, to witness the truth for yourselves.'

Holly whistled softly. '*Can* you?'

'I never have tried. Never had cause. It might come to naught. But then again . . .' She blinked and shook her head, as if shaking something off. 'I think perhaps 'tis the only way. If you are willing.'

'I am,' said Holly firmly.

'It will not be pleasant,' Susannah warned.

'Maybe not. But it can't be worse than not knowing, can it, Tom?' Holly waited for an answer. 'Tom?'

'No,' said Tom, then swallowed, and mentally strengthened his nerve. 'No, it can't.'

'Very well,' said Susannah, 'then come; stand by me and we shall try.'

They moved to stand beside her. Was the air just a

little colder where Susannah was? Tom wondered, and pushed the thought hurriedly away.

Susannah said: 'Reach out your hands towards the mill.'

They obeyed. Tom's fingers were itching, and Holly kept flexing hers as though they ached. Susannah positioned herself between them, then stretched out her own hands and laid them one on Holly's left hand and the other on Tom's right.

Tom didn't know what to expect as the ghost's fingers made contact with his. An icy shock? A hot tingling? In fact, he felt nothing at all, not the smallest sensation of any kind. He wondered if Holly was experiencing the same, but he didn't dare look at her, let alone ask.

'Good,' Susannah said. 'Now, shut your eyes.'

Tom had a lurch of vertigo as he closed his eyes tightly, but it passed after a couple of seconds. He thought he heard the swish of Susannah's long skirt as she moved a little. Then she said, 'Walk forward seven steps. Then look again.'

'We're too close to the edge of the bank—' Tom started to object, but Holly cut across him. 'Shut up, Tom, and do as she says!'

Slowly, and wondering if he was making a very dangerous mistake, Tom walked forward. 'One,' he said aloud. 'Two.'

'Count *quietly*!' Holly hissed.

Three paces, four, five, six . . . he expected to pitch

headlong off the bank at any moment, but it didn't happen. Seven . . .

A sharp pain shot through the hand that Susannah was holding, as though someone had stuck a dozen needles into him. Tom jerked his hand back, then opened his eyes.

Susannah was gone. Holly stood beside him, looking a bit fazed. They were still on the bank, still a couple of paces from the edge, though Tom couldn't for the life of him work out how. The sun was no longer shining, and everything was absolutely silent. Below them, Trevenna Mill spread and sprawled on its grassy plateau.

But it was Trevenna Mill as they had never, ever seen it before.

10

The silence broke suddenly in a headlong rush that filled Tom's ears with noise. The first thing he heard clearly was the rain. It was pouring down, pooling and puddling on the ground and saturating everything. Yet Tom could not feel it. It was as if he stood inside an invisible bubble, looking out at another world.

Then other sounds started to separate out, and he realized that the water noise wasn't only the rain. There was a stronger splashing, like a fast-flowing current, and over that came a great clattering and rumbling from the mill itself. The ancient building was no longer a ruin. The millwheel was whole again, revolving steadily in the torrent of water that tumbled and piled through the race. And deep inside the building, the huge mechanism of shafts and cogs was turning the great grinding stones as the mill did its work.

Tom stared numbly. Where the overgrown garden should have been, two empty carts stood in a bare yard. A piebald horse was in the shafts of one cart, head down and mane and tail dripping as it stood resignedly in the wet. Chickens skittered about, and three geese splashed in one of the largest puddles.

A hand on his arm broke the spell on Tom, and he

turned to see Holly pointing behind them. He looked. The millpond, which he knew only as an empty hollow, was brim full of water, like a huge, gloomily shining mirror. At the pond's far end the sluice-gates were open. The stream poured out through a channel that carried it surging down the bank and into the stone-lined millrace.

Holly said in a small voice, 'It was sunny just now . . .'

'I know. And it was the twenty-first century . . .'

'Then w . . . we've come back. To Susannah's time. We're seeing what happened . . .'

They both stood staring at the scene, half-convinced that they must be dreaming. Then there was a quick movement at one side of the mill and a small boy appeared, with a smaller girl hurrying after him. They were both dressed in old-fashioned clothes, and the little girl wore an apron and cap like Susannah's.

Holly drew in a sharp breath. 'Those children – they must be—'

A voice said, 'The boy is my brother Peter, and the girl my sister Eliza.'

Tom and Holly started almost out of their skins as Susannah appeared between them. Her face was paler than ever and her eyes were huge and dark as she gazed down at the two running children. Then a third child appeared, an even younger girl, barely older than Katy, and Susannah's voice caught with emotion as she added, 'There is Ruth. She is – was – the youngest of us all.'

Tom stood speechless as they all watched the three

children run on across the yard and disappear through the door of the mill. Then Susannah spoke again.

'We had had almost no rain that summer, and the winter and spring had been dry, too. The millstream was weak and fed little water to the pond; sometimes the race was hardly strong enough to turn the wheel. Father was greatly concerned. So he made a plan to use the rest of the stream—'

'The rest of it?' Holly interrupted, curious. 'What do you mean?'

'Ah, of course; you would not know. When milling first began here, only a part of the stream was sent to the millpond. The rest of it ran on down the valley, as it had always done. Father made a new channel to take all the water, so that the mill would not fail.'

'And the rest of the stream – the old course – dried up?'

Susannah nodded, and her face became tight and pinched. 'Father didn't know what he had done. He didn't even know that *it* was there. None of us knew. How could we have done? How could we have known that the stream was its home . . . ?'

The first inkling of the truth began to creep up on Tom and Holly. 'What is *it* . . . ?' Tom asked.

She shuddered. 'A spirit. A demon. An unholy thing of water and darkness . . .' She shut her eyes, shivering again. 'It is full of anger and hatred, and it hated us above all others, for we had destroyed its home. We didn't *know* . . .'

She covered her face with both hands in distress, then with a visible effort controlled herself and looked down at the mill again.

'I remember this day so well,' she went on more quietly. 'It was the fourth day after the rain began. The millpond had filled quickly because of the new stream, and Father said that before long we should open the other gate to let out the excess. He was greatly relieved. And then . . . then, I saw it for the first time.'

The scene below them wavered as if the world had suddenly been plunged under water. Tom rubbed his eyes, trying to clear them. Then everything stabilized again. The horse and cart had gone, and Susannah was no longer beside them. Instead, a solitary figure carrying a bowl and wearing a cape and hood over her dress was hurrying past the millrace in the rain. Halfway across the yard she stopped, and stared at the turning millwheel as if transfixed.

'It's Susannah!' Holly whispered. 'And look — there, behind the wheel —'

Even at this distance they could see it. Hunched, lurking, the crone-like figure squatted on the ledge in the wheel's shadow. There was a clatter as Susannah dropped her bowl in shock, and she screamed shrilly. Other figures came running: a plump woman, two of the children they had seen before, and a boy of sixteen or so. They gathered round her and she pointed to the race.

But the crone was gone.

The image wavered again, and the figures in the yard faded out. 'They did not believe me.' Susannah was beside them again. 'Father said I was mazed and Mother thought I must be sick of a fever. But I saw it well enough. And I felt its evil.'

'Did any of your family ever see it?' asked Holly.

'Yes. For it came again and again. The summer changed, and after all the dryness there was barely a day without rain. The rain fed it and gave it strength. John saw it first. Then Peter and Ruth. Ruth was so frightened that she cried all night and nothing could console her. Then one day Mother and I were feeding the chickens when it appeared once more. Mother near fainted away. She had been angry with John and me, for she thought we had made up the story to fright the little ones.'

'But she believed you after that,' said Tom.

'Oh, yes. Oh, yes. She felt the evil of it, just as we did. She ran to Father and begged him to fetch Parson to banish it. But Father would not.' Susannah swallowed. 'He said twas heathen superstition and unseemly in a Christian household, and he wouldn't shame himself by calling on Parson.'

'So nothing was done . . .' Holly murmured. 'What happened then, Susannah?'

Susannah's fists clenched at her sides. 'I can't say more,' she replied at last. 'Not with words. You must see for yourselves now.' She moved to the edge of the bank. 'But you must make a promise. Whatever you see or hear, don't interfere, for 'tisn't your proper place. Say no word to any but each other. And do nothing *at all*.' She stared hard at them. 'It is the past, and the past can't be changed. So promise.'

'I promise,' said Holly.

'Me, too,' said Tom.

Susannah studied them both for a few moments, trying to decide if she could trust them. At last she nodded. 'Very well. Follow me.'

She set off down the bank, and after a second's hesitation Tom and Holly went after her. She moved more quickly than they could on the steep, uneven slope, and they were only halfway down by the time she reached the bottom. As she reached it her figure became vague and grey, as if she was fading. Tom squinted, wondering if it was a trick of the light. But everything around her was fading too, blanking out and blinding him like a dense fog. He stopped, disorientated – and abruptly the scene snapped back into focus.

Susannah had disappeared, and so had the chickens and the geese. But the millwheel still turned, and machinery rumbled inside the mill. It was still raining, too, though less heavily and, again, they couldn't feel it.

Tom gazed around. 'It all looks different. And it's so quiet. Where is everyone?'

'I think I know,' said Holly. 'It's a different time of day. The light's going; it's nearly dusk. The mill's working, but they'll have put the children to bed and shut the chickens and geese up for the night.'

Tom looked at the water wheel. 'That race is going at quite a speed.'

'Mmm. Scary, isn't it? The sheer power of that water; when you think—'

She didn't get any further because Tom grabbed her arm. 'Shh! Look!'

'What?' Holly spun round. Two children had appeared from the direction of the house and were approaching the race.

'It's Eliza and Ruth,' Holly whispered. 'Move – quick, before they see us!'

'They'd have seen us by now if they could,' said Tom. 'We must be invisible.' He frowned. 'There's something weird about them. Something wrong . . .'

The two little girls were both wearing long white shifts with woollen shawls around their shoulders. Despite the weather they were barefoot and bare-headed, and they walked slowly, unsteadily, almost as though they were groping their way along in the dark.

'They look as if they're hypnotized,' whispered Holly. 'Or asleep . . .'

Tom's eyes widened. 'You're right – they *are* asleep! Look at their faces; they're blank, just staring into space!'

'Sleepwalking . . .' Holly breathed. 'And look where they're heading!'

The children were stumbling towards the millrace, and

with an awful sense of premonition Tom and Holly looked at the wheel.

The crone was there. It crouched on the ledge, absolutely still. A spider in a deadly web, waiting for its prey.

'It's got them under its control,' Holly whispered, horrified. 'It's bringing them to it, just the way it brought me . . .'

'We've got to warn them!' Tom started forward, but she gripped his arm.

'No! Remember what Susannah said? We can't change the past, Tom. This *happened*.'

He couldn't argue with her, but he felt sick with fear and pity for the two little girls as they stumbled closer and closer to the danger. The thing on the ledge had started to move now, swaying slightly from side to side, becoming excited. Tom couldn't bear to look and shut his eyes. Then from the direction of the house someone called.

'Eliza! Ruth! Where are you?'

Susannah came into view. She was breathless, soaking wet and very agitated. 'Eliza! Ruth!' She ran straight past Tom and Holly, then saw the girls.

'No!' Her voice rose shrilly over the splash and rumble of the water wheel. 'Oh, dear God, *no*! Father, Mother, John – come *quickly*!'

Eliza and Ruth had reached the stone pile that supported the bridge over the millrace. With a dreadful determination they started to climb up. Screaming again for her parents, brother, *anyone*, Susannah raced after them. Then more running footsteps sounded, and a boy a year or so older than her appeared.

'Sussa, what's to do?'

'The girls, John – it's trying to take the girls! Where's Father?'

'In the mill; it'll take too long to fetch him! But Daniel's here; he's just brought the chairs he's mended for Mother—'

'There isn't time to fetch him! Help me!' Susannah hurled herself at the bank and started after her sisters, who had reached the bridge. John hesitated a bare moment, then tore after her. Slipping and slithering in the rain they scrambled up. Susannah reached the top first; Eliza and Ruth were crossing the bridge and she followed, her shoes clattering hollowly on the wooden planks. She reached them when they were halfway across, and the bridge quivered and shook as she snatched hold of little Ruth and made a grab for Eliza. But the children resisted, and though Susannah was bigger and stronger, she couldn't control them both.

'John, help me!' she wailed.

Her brother raced to join her, grasped hold of Ruth and started to carry her back over the bridge. Suddenly there were new noises; feet running, a man shouting, a woman's cry of alarm. The miller himself, John Hoskin, had appeared at the mill door, and from the house came his wife, a young man and two more children. The miller pelted towards the bridge. He was up the bank like a mountain goat; the younger John all but hurled little Ruth into his arms, then went back to help Susannah with the struggling Eliza.

From the wheel came a scream of rage that pierced the air and stopped everyone in their tracks. It seemed to jolt Eliza out of her trance, for suddenly she wasn't struggling any more but was clinging desperately to Susannah. Even from a distance Tom and Holly could hear her wails of terror.

'Bring her away!' the miller yelled. '*Hurry!*'

John took Eliza from Susannah and they ran back to the end of the bridge. Mrs Hoskin and Daniel had reached the bank by now, and the children were handed down to them. Then John turned to look back across the bridge.

'Run, Susannah!' he shouted. '*Run!*'

Susannah was alone in the middle of the bridge; she turned to obey – and what happened then stunned Tom and Holly to the core. From behind the revolving wheel, a shape moved with impossible speed. It launched itself through the churning cascade of water, lunged across the bridge, and a dark, flapping form like a monstrous bat fastened on Susannah. Susannah shrieked; then she and the monstrosity were swaying together on the bridge, locked in a wild, flailing combat.

'*Sussa!*' the younger John screamed. He pounded back

to the bridge, his father and older brother at his heels –

But they were too late. Susannah lost her footing and fell heavily against the bridge's wooden rail. Tom glimpsed, again, the hideous, green-white face, twisted in triumph as the bridge rail broke and Susannah fell straight on to the turning millwheel.

'No-o-o!' Tom heard his own voice go up in a wavering moan that mingled with the screams of the Hoskins, as Susannah's thrashing body disappeared into the wheel's crushing paddles. For a moment the wheel churned inexorably on – then an enormous jolt went through Tom. The scene froze, warped . . . and vanished. he was on his hands and knees on dry grass, in daylight. The sun was shining. And the only sounds were birdsong, and Dublin barking distantly in the house.

Slowly Tom raised his head. He felt sick and dizzy, and all his muscles ached. Holly was a few paces away. She was still on her feet, but her face had turned grey and her mouth hung open as she stared blankly at the still, silent mill.

A few seconds passed, then Holly said softly, 'Now we know . . .'

Tom stood up unsteadily. There were awful images in his head, and the worst one of all was the memory of the broken bones he and his father had unearthed inside the mill. The power of the race, the speed of the wheel . . . he swallowed hard as he imagined what the combination could do to a human body.

Suddenly Holly came over to him, put her arms round his neck and hugged him. He hugged her back. There wasn't anything he could say that did not seem stupid and pointless.

'Let's go indoors,' he got out at last. 'I think I'd like to sit down for a bit.'

She nodded wordlessly and they walked towards the house.

They turned the corner, and Susannah was standing in front of them.

For several seconds they stared at each other, until Holly broke the silence.

'Oh, Susannah . . .' she said. 'I'm so sorry.'

Susannah looked down at the ground. Tom was slightly freaked to see her looking so normal – well, he amended, as normal as a ghost could be – when only a few minutes ago . . . He hastily blanked that thought and mumbled that he was sorry, too.

'Was that . . .' Holly gulped, tried again. 'Was that why your family left the mill?'

'Yes,' said Susannah. She sighed. 'There is more to tell. But I think this is not a good time. For now, you have seen enough.'

Though he was ashamed of himself, Tom wholeheartedly agreed, and even the strong-willed Holly nodded faintly.

'Then I will find another way to finish my story,' said Susannah. 'I think I can. Tonight, perhaps. In a dream.'

'You can influence dreams?' Holly asked in astonishment.

'I think so. I will try. And now I must go.'

She turned and started to walk away, and belatedly Tom remembered something. 'Susannah, wait a moment!' he called.

But Susannah was no longer there.

'We didn't tell her about the American family . . .' Tom said.

'She didn't give us time.' Holly blinked at the empty space where Susannah had been.

'Right. God, I feel weird . . .'

'Me, too. Look, I think we should do something. Go for a walk, go to the village, play with Dublin – anything that'll make us feel normal again.'

Tom nearly said, '*Normal?*' but checked himself. 'Yeah. Yeah, OK. That's probably the most sensible idea either of us is going to come up with.'

'And tonight, one of us is going to dream. I wonder which one it'll be . . .'

He shivered. 'I just hope we can get to sleep. It's not going to be easy, if we're expecting something like . . .' he waved a hand towards the millwheel, '. . . like *that*.'

'We've got to try, though. Not just for Susannah, but for ourselves, too.' Holly paused. 'For everyone.'

11

Tom tried everything he could think of to stay awake that night. He read, he played mental games, he listened to music on his headphones; any trick at all. All right, it was cowardly, and he was trying to pass the buck to Holly. But he was deeply afraid of what he might see in his dreams.

The attempt didn't work, though. By one a.m. he was sound asleep. And the dream Susannah had promised came.

It wasn't like a dream in the usual sense, and it was nothing like as frightening as Tom had feared. At the end of it he woke, quite calm, to find the first hint of daylight coming in at his window and the dawn chorus going full strength outside. He sat up in bed. He had expected to remember the dream clearly, but he didn't. The scenes and images – if there had been any – were gone. But he knew with absolute certainty the rest of Susannah's story.

It was a pitiful tale. The horror of what had happened to their eldest daughter had thrown the family into shock. But even worse was the knowledge of why she had died. The thing that haunted the mill had murdered her, and they had all seen it happen. Even Miller Hoskin couldn't doubt the monstrosity's existence now – and he was more frightened than anyone.

What they did then would have seemed barbaric in modern times. But this family had lived two hundred years ago, and a combination of fear, panic and superstition swamped them. They told no one of Susannah's death. Instead, in a desperate attempt to appease the demon, they had 'given' it Susannah's body, burying her behind a wall in the mill as a kind of primitive offering. Then they had packed their belongings and all the money they could muster, and fled. Daniel, the married son who had been visiting on that fateful night, abandoned his wife without a word of explanation and went with them. None of them ever returned.

When the Hoskins could not be traced, Trevenna Mill was sold. But the new owners stayed only a few months before they sold up again, and three more owners did the same. At last the mill closed for good, and that was how it had been for nearly two hundred years. Now and then someone had bought the property and lived in the house for a while, but none of them stayed long before moving away. Tom's family were just the latest in a long line.

Susannah had seen all this happen. Tom now knew why her spirit had stayed at the mill since she died. The stream, as Susannah had said, was the demon's home, and when Miller Hoskin diverted it to run the mill more efficiently, the demon had been trapped in the new water course. So in revenge it had killed Susannah and ensnared her spirit; she was caught in its power, and she could not leave unless it chose to let her go.

Which it would only do if it had a new victim to take her place . . .

Only the fact that it was five o'clock in the morning stopped Tom from grabbing his mobile and phoning Holly. If she, too, had had the dream then she would already know what he knew. But if she hadn't, he needed to tell her everything as soon as he could – because a terrible thought had occurred to him. Susannah only had to lure some unsuspecting person into the demon's grasp, and there would be a new victim to set her free. So far, her conscience had been too great for her to do that; in fact she had tried to keep them out of its clutches, which said a lot about the sort of person she was. But the temptation must be enormous. So if she felt bitter towards her family for running away and leaving her to the demon's mercy, then when the American descendants arrived, that temptation might just be too much to resist.

Unable to lie in bed any longer, Tom got up, dressed quickly and went downstairs. Dublin greeted him joyfully, and Tom clipped the dog's lead on and took him out and down the valley path. He wanted to get away from the mill, to avoid meeting Susannah in case she picked up what was in his mind – and he needed to give himself time to think.

Five minutes later his mobile rang.

'Tom, it's me,' said Holly. 'I'm really sorry if I woke you up, but I couldn't wait any longer.'

Tom laughed hollowly. 'You didn't wake me up,' he told her. 'I'm halfway to the creek, with Dublin. Couldn't sleep.'

'Ah. Then you dreamed it, too?'

Relief rushed through him as he realized that he wasn't going to have to explain it all to her. 'Yeah,' he said. 'The lot. Including the reason why Susannah can't escape from here.'

'I know. It's so scary. And I keep thinking about the New England people.'

'Oh, hell,' said Tom. 'You're telepathic. Either that, or it's just howlingly obvious. What are we going to *do*?'

'Is there any way you can stop them from coming?'

'What, you mean go to Mum and Dad and say, "You'd better not let the Redmays come, because there's a demon in the mill that'll try to kill them, and a ghost that might help?" Get real!'

'All right, all right! That's out. But there's got to be *something*.'

'Maybe we should just tell Susannah and she how she reacts.'

'We were going to tell her yesterday, but we didn't. Mightn't it be better to keep quiet? I mean, we've left it a bit late . . .'

'If we don't tell her, and they turn up and she realizes

152

who they are, that could be a whole lot worse,' Tom pointed out.

'But if she doesn't realize, then it's probably safer not to tell her.'

'Yeah, I know. It's a gamble either way, isn't it?' His phone suddenly made an appalling noise and Tom stopped walking. 'The signal's breaking up; I'm probably getting too far down the valley. Look, I know it's Sunday and you've got church and all that, but can we get together later on?'

'I think we'd better,' Holly agreed. 'And make a few decisions.' She paused. 'I'll come up by boat after lunch. Meet me at the jetty at . . . say, two-thirty.'

'OK. See you.' Tom broke the connection and stood indecisively on the path. He didn't feel like walking any more. In fact he didn't feel like doing anything at all except going to sleep, then waking up to find that all his problems had magically disappeared and everything was all right again.

That, though, wasn't going to happen. He looked down the path ahead of him. Then he looked back towards the mill. He didn't want to be there right now.

'Come on, Dublin.' He gathered up the lead again. 'Walkies.'

Dublin yelped ecstatically and, wishing he could be as carefree as the dog, Tom walked on down the valley.

Tom went home in time to pretend he had only just

got up, so that suspicions wouldn't be raised. Mrs McCarthy had a beginner pupil that morning, so for an hour the house was full of discordant noises that were only slightly better than the din Katy made whenever she could sneak into the piano-room. Afterwards Mum said she was going to check her e-mail, so Tom and his father made lunch. Tom was clattering plates on to the table when Mum came in looking enthusiastic.

'I've had another message from Jane Redmay,' she said. 'They certainly don't believe in wasting any time! They're flying to England next week, and they'll be coming to visit us the week after.'

Tom's face froze and Dad said, 'How many of them?'

'Jane and her husband, Bob, and their three children.'

He looked dismayed. 'They're not expecting to stay here, are they?'

'Don't be daft!' said Mum. 'I told them the house is totally uncivilized, and anyway they've already got it all organized. They've booked a couple of nights at a hotel in Falmouth.' She beamed at Tom. 'The week after next's your half-term, isn't it?'

'Er . . . yes,' said Tom.

'Then they couldn't have timed it better.'

'No,' said Tom. 'They couldn't, could they?'

Holly's boat was coming up the creek when Tom arrived at the jetty. She took one look at his face and said, 'What's happened?'

He told her about the Redmays' message. '*That* soon?' she said. 'Oh, no!'

'Exactly. So we've got to decide fast. Do we tell Susannah, or do we keep quiet and hope nothing goes horribly wrong?'

Holly kicked off her sandals, climbed out of the boat and waded ashore. 'I've been thinking, and I reckon we should tell her.' She secured the mooring rope and gave it a jerk to make sure it was fast. 'Think what she did yesterday. Showing us all those scenes from the past, then sending us both the dream. She's got abilities way beyond ordinary humans', so there's no way she isn't going to know who the Redmays are, is there?'

'Good point.'

'And if she's going to know,' Holly continued, 'what about the demon? It's sure to spot them a mile off. We've *got* to tell her, Tom, and we've got to persuade her not to be angry. Because it's a pretty sure bet that we're going to need her help!'

She was right, and there was no point trying to find a way round it. 'OK,' said Tom heavily. 'So let's get up to the mill and get it over with.'

They agreed that the best way to make contact with Susannah was to do exactly what they had done yesterday; call to her and hope that she would be willing to appear. They would have to be careful, for Tom's mother and Katy were in the garden and banging noises from the mill building told them that Mr McCarthy was inside. But they managed to find a private spot, and called Susannah's name.

Nothing happened. They repeated the call several times, then moved on to another spot and tried again. But Susannah did not come.

'This is useless,' Holly said at last. 'Either she can't answer or she won't.'

'It's "won't", if you ask me,' said Tom gloomily. 'I bet you anything she's found out and she's furious with us.'

'Don't say that! It's more likely because your mum and dad are around and she doesn't want to risk them seeing her. We'll leave it till they go indoors, then try again.'

Mr and Mrs McCarthy were determined to make the most of the fine weather, and before long Tom and Holly were given gloves, forks and hoes and roped into helping with the gardening. It passed the time, if nothing else, but it was nearly six o'clock by the time they had the chance to try and contact Susannah a second time.

It didn't work. Susannah did not show up and nothing they did made any difference. Eventually they gave up and Holly said she must go home. Tom felt discouraged and worried, but he promised that he would keep trying.

He did try again that night in his room, but he had no more luck than before. Whatever her reasons, Susannah was staying well away from him. He wondered if perhaps after yesterday she was too upset, or exhausted, or both, to face him again. He hoped that was the case, because the alternative – that she already knew about the Redmays' visit and was angry that she had not been told – didn't bear thinking about. All he could do was be patient, stay alert, and hope that she would relent before too long.

Nearly a week later Susannah still hadn't relented. And then the weather changed.

It started with two days of gloomy TV forecasts, then on the third day the rain began. Tom woke in the middle of the night to hear it drumming on the roof and rushing and gurgling in the gutters, and when he tried to look outside all he could see was a solid slide of water streaming down the panes of his window.

'Ye gods' Mrs McCarthy said at breakfast the next morning. 'Just *look* at it!' The garden was all but blanked out, and the downpour showed no signs of relenting.

'The gutters are overflowing already; you can hear them upstairs,' said Tom's father. 'We'll be borrowing Holly's boat at this rate.'

'I know. And the Redmays are flying in tonight. What a welcome to Britain!'

'You all right, Tom?' Dad asked, seeing Tom's face fall.

'What? Oh – er – yeah; I'm fine.' But he wasn't. *The Redmays are flying in tonight.* Another few days and they would be here at the mill . . .

'Fat chance of this letting up,' Mr McCarthy went on. 'I'll drive you to the school bus stop, or you'll be half drowned before you get there.'

'Er . . . yeah, thanks, Dad.' But getting soaked on the way to school was the least of Tom's worries. All he could think about was that he couldn't make contact with Susannah, and that the weather would give power to the demon . . . *Stop raining*! he prayed silently. *Please, just stop!*

As the thought went through his mind, thunder grumbled far in the distance. It was as if some unkind spirit had heard him and was laughing up its sleeve.

And he had an awful feeling that this was only the beginning.

The Redmays rang the following day. Apparently, said Mrs McCarthy when she came off the phone, they were quite philosophical about the weather and were determined not to let it stop their visit to Cornwall.

'They've hired a car,' she added, 'and they'll be visiting us on Monday – first day of your half-term, Tom.'

'Right,' said Tom, his spirits sinking. The weather had shown no sign whatever of letting up, and the forecast was for more of the same. He couldn't *believe* it was nearly June. And he couldn't stop the feeling that some power beyond human control just might have engineered the whole thing to turn out this way.

The only spark of hope on the horizon was his

mother's suggestion that Holly might like to come over to Trevenna, meet the Redmays and stay for dinner with them all in the evening. Holly accepted at once – but she shared Tom's fears.

'This weather's going to get worse if anything,' she said worriedly. 'It's giving the demon all the opportunity it could possibly want. Tom, are you *sure* you've tried everything you can think of to make contact with Susannah?'

'Short of killing myself so I can go over to the other side and grab her, yes!' Tom said with feeling.

'OK, sorry; it was a dumb question. But if you *could* try again . . .'

'Last desperate attempt? All right. Though I don't think it'll do any good.'

He was right; it didn't. The rain continued on and off all through the weekend, and still Susannah would not show herself. But at least the weather stopped the McCarthys from venturing outside unless they absolutely had to, so no one was likely to stray within reach of the thing in the millrace. All the same, Tom was as jumpy as a flea when Monday dawned – wet – and he waited for the Redmays and Holly to arrive.

Holly got there first. She had come up the creek in the boat – quicker than walking, she said, and though the creek was swollen, the current wasn't too strong. All the same, her waterproof was streaming and her hair dripping. Mrs McCarthy fussed over her, asking if she wanted a change of clothes, and Holly was in the middle of politely refusing when the sound of a car engine announced the arrival of the Redmays.

In seconds the kitchen was a chaos of greetings, talk, laughter and puddles that pooled on the tiled floor as coats were peeled off and everybody introduced themselves to everyone else. Jane and Bob Redmay were about the same age as Tom's parents, and their three children – Robbie, Chelsea and Jack – ranged in age from thirteen down to six. Robbie, the eldest, was quiet and shy, with a pleasant smile; Chelsea was pretty, and knew it, and obviously didn't think much of Cornwall. Jack, the six-year-old, was a bundle of energy, with fair hair and a lot of freckles and a very loud voice. Unlike his sister he thought the mill was really cool, and he wanted to explore every centimetre of it, right *now*.

He had to wait, though, because first there was tea, or Coke, and some cakes, while everyone made the sort of small-talk that people do when they are first getting to know each other. They talked about homes and families and work and school – and, of course, the weather. According to Bob Redmay the road into the village was nearly awash, and when they drove over the humpbacked bridge the water running under it had looked more like a raging torrent than a small stream.

'The millpond's back to being a mini-lake already,' Tom's father said. 'Mind you, once it gets over a certain level, the water goes out through the old overflow channel and back to the stream. Still, we'd better keep an eye on it.'

They talked on for a few more minutes, then Jack couldn't wait any longer and begged to see over the mill.

'Come on, then,' said Mr McCarthy with a grin. 'The rain isn't going to let up, so we might as well go now as later.'

'Cool!' Jack yelled triumphantly. 'C'mon, Dad, Mom! I want to see *everything*!'

Tom and Holly lent their waterproofs and Mrs McCarthy found a couple of spare ones. Chelsea, though, said she didn't want to get wet again and would rather stay in the house. So her family trooped off with Tom's parents, Katy and Dublin for a tour of the mill, and when they had gone there was an uncomfortable silence as Tom and Holly tried to think of something friendly to say.

'Do you want another Coke?' Tom asked at last.

'No.' Chelsea shook her head.

'Oh. Well, there's—'

'Can I go to the bathroom?'

Holly turned away to hide her expression, and Tom said, 'Sure. It's upstairs, then turn—'

'I know. Your mom showed we when we got here.' She went out without another word and they heard her feet thumping up the staircase.

Holly pulled a face. 'Hi, Chelsea, great to know you, too!'

Tom grinned. 'She reminds me of you the first time we met.'

'Oh, shut up! Seriously, while she's out of the way, we need to talk. Is your mother going to tell them about Susannah?'

'She said she is, probably later when we all eat. But she's a bit worried about it; you know, how they'll take it and everything.'

'Mmm.' Holly was silent for a few moments. Then: 'I'm worried, too. About Jack.'

'Why? He's OK.'

'Oh, yes; he's a nice kid. That's not the problem. It's his energy.' Holly nodded at the window, through which they could see Jack tearing round the garden while the others waited by the mill entrance. 'He's into everything, exploring everything, and he's totally fearless. He could run straight into danger, and he won't be easy to watch. If he was Katy's age, fine, but—'

Tom thought he heard a noise, thought it was Chelsea coming back, and said hastily, 'Shh!' He turned round, ready to say something in another effort to be pleasant – and froze.

Chelsea hadn't come back. But Susannah had.

12

'Send them away!' Tom and Holly had never heard Susannah sound so wild and angry before. 'You should never have let them come!'

'Susannah—' Holly began.

'*Send them away!*'

'We can't!' Tom said desperately. 'We didn't invite them, and we can't make them go!'

'You must!' Susannah's outline wavered alarmingly. 'I know who they are, and I do not *want* them here! They left me; they went away and they left me alone and trapped and – and –' The words collapsed and she started to sob. It was a horrible thing to see a ghost crying; her face crumpled and her mouth worked, but she made no sound at all.

'Susannah,' Holly said with a huge surge of compassion, 'they're not the same people who went away and left you. They – your family – they're all gone now. They're . . .' She couldn't bring herself to say the word *dead*. She swallowed. 'They're not the same.'

Susannah's sobbing stopped as quickly as it had started, which was even more unnerving. She stared at them both, and suddenly everything about her looked grey.

Then: 'Send them away,' she said. 'Or I cannot answer for what will happen.'

'What do you mean?' Tom asked in alarm.

'What I say. I cannot answer for it. You must send them away. Before it's too late.'

And the next instant, she wasn't there any more.

'Susannah!' Tom gasped. He started forward, grabbing at the empty air where Susannah had been – and as he did so, the kitchen door opened and Chelsea Redmay appeared.

Chelsea stopped on the threshold and Tom did his best to look as if he hadn't been doing anything in particular. 'Hi . . .' he said weakly. 'Did you find the bathroom OK?'

She didn't answer that. Instead, she asked, 'Who's Susannah?'

Tom gawped like a landed fish, but Holly cut in quickly, 'Sue who?' she said, looking vague and innocent.

Chelsea eyed her shrewdly. 'You were calling someone. You said, "Susannah". I heard you.'

Tom had recovered his wits. 'Oh, we were just talking about someone at school. Weren't we, Holly?'

'Yeah,' Holly agreed. Chelsea's gaze flicked from one to the other of them, and Tom noticed that the American girl's manner had changed. The air of bored confidence had suddenly disappeared, and in its place was a curiosity tinged with suspicion. Surely, he thought, Chelsea hadn't realized? The door had been shut; she couldn't possibly have seen Susannah.

Unless Susannah had made herself visible on her way to the kitchen . . .

Abruptly Chelsea said, 'Do you have another waterproof?'

'What? Oh – er, yes, in the hall.'

'OK. Then I'll go join Mom and Dad.' Another flicking look, and this time the suspicion was very obvious. She hesitated, as if she was about to say something else, then changed her mind and hurried out of the kitchen.

'Whoo!' said Holly. 'What's got into her? You don't think –'

'I don't know, but I wouldn't mind betting she's picked up something. And after what Susannah said . . .'

'Yeah. Look, I think we'd better go and join the party, too. Keep an eye on things; just in case.'

Tom agreed. Chelsea had already gone, and they went after her, ducking into the rain and sprinting the distance. The Redmays and Tom's parents were in the depths of the mill by now, looking at the massive shafts and cogs that had linked up the water wheel to turn the grinding stones. Bob Redmay was examining the stones, saying wonderingly how powerful the millrace must have been to turn all that huge machinery. Robbie, the elder boy, was standing watching and listening, while Jack was scrambling over everything that he was allowed to, saying 'Wow!' and 'Cool!' and 'Hey, Dad, come look at this!' every few seconds.

Tom's mum, though, was having trouble with Katy.

'She keeps trying to run outside again,' she told Tom. 'She says it's nasty and she doesn't want to stay here because of something; I don't know what, but she's got a real bee in her bonnet. Take her back to the house, would you, love, and stay with her?'

Katy was clinging to her mother's coat, her face red and screwed up as if she was about to have a full-scale tantrum. Tom couldn't argue. He took his sister's hand and said, 'Come on, Kitten-Kat. We'll play indoors.'

'Dubly come too!' Katy insisted. 'Want Dubly!'

'All right, we'll take him with us. Come on.'

Dublin wasn't so keen on leaving, but Tom held him by the collar and pulled him along. At the door he glanced back. Bob and his father were still examining the millstones. Holly was keeping an eye on Jack. His mother was talking to Jane.

And Chelsea, on her own in a corner, was staring at him very hard indeed.

The rain stopped soon afterwards, which was just as well because the complete mill tour took hours. The Redmays were fascinated by what they jokingly called their 'ancestral home' and had insisted on seeing every bit of it, even including a look at the rapidly-filling millpond. Jack was firmly stopped from fiddling around the excavations where the sluice-gates had been, but even so he managed to get muddy enough for his own satisfaction.

Mrs McCarthy had planned dinner early, so the guests could get away at a reasonable time. There were plenty of willing hands to help, and while Katy was put to bed everyone pitched in to get the meal ready.

Or almost everyone. They realized Jack was missing as the table was being laid.

'Where's he got to?' Bob Redmay asked.

'The millpond,' said Robbie. 'You can bet on it.'

'That kid . . .' Muttering darkly, Bob went outside, and moments later they heard him shout, 'Jack! Come down here this minute!'

Exchanging a quick look, Tom and Holly followed Bob out. Jack was scrambling down the bank, looking sheepish and a bit guilty.

'What were you doing up there?' his father demanded.

Jack shrugged. 'Just taking another look at that gate thing, you know?' His face was furtive. 'I didn't touch it.'

'You'd better not have, or you'll be hearing from Mom and me! Now go get cleaned up!' The small boy ran off and Bob smiled an apology at Tom. 'Sorry, Tom. But I don't suppose he hurt anything up there.'

'Don't worry.' Tom was relieved; his only concern was that Jack might have strayed too near the millrace. 'There's not much for him to hurt, anyway.'

He looked at the millrace as they went back into the house, but nothing moved on the ledge beyond the wheel. That in itself was worrying. It made him wonder if the demon was biding its time, waiting for the right moment to strike. *Well*, he told himself, *we'll just have to make sure the right moment doesn't come.*

And Jack would have to be watched very carefully indeed.

Katy had, for once, gone to sleep without any trouble, so a few minutes later everyone sat down to eat. Mrs McCarthy waited until the main course was nearly finished before she said.

'Bob . . . Jane . . . there's one thing we haven't told you about Trevenna Mill yet, and that I think you ought to know.' She paused. 'It's about the skeleton.'

The Redmays all said, 'Skeleton?' and Jack added, 'Wow! Where?'

Tom's mother told the story of the bones in the wall. As the visitors listened, Tom and Holly watched carefully for reactions. Bob, Jane and Robbie were fascinated, and didn't seem the least bit freaked. Jack, predictably, thought the whole thing was really cool, and wanted to know if there might be any more skeletons they hadn't dug up yet. Chelsea was just quiet. Very quiet.

'. . . So there was a proper funeral for her at the village church,' Mrs McCarthy finished, 'and that's really the end of the story.'

'Poor girl,' said Jane compassionately. 'I hope she's at rest now.' She sighed. 'What a thing to have happened! No wonder her family – my family – emigrated.'

They didn't seem to think that murder might have been involved; maybe, Tom thought, because they didn't want to contemplate it. Then suddenly Chelsea spoke.

'What was the girl's name, Mrs McCarthy?'

'We don't know,' Tom's mother told her. 'The Hoskins had four daughters, but there's no way of telling if she was one of them. She could have been anyone.'

Chelsea nodded. Then, looking directly, challengingly at Tom, she said, 'Was she called Susannah?'

Tom felt as if someone had shoved a red-hot needle into the base of his spine. He tried frantically to think of something to say, but his mother beat him to it.

'It's strange you should say that, because one of the Hoskin girls *was* called Susannah. Holly found it in the parish records, didn't you, Holly? However did you come up with that name, Chelsea?'

'Something I heard.' Chelsea was still staring at Tom, and was obviously about to add something more when Holly cut in quickly.

'Uh-oh,' she said. 'Look at that sky!'

Heads turned to the kitchen window. From being just grey and rainy the sky had turned an ominous purplish-black. The light in the garden — what there was of it — looked eerie and unnatural, and everyone realized how dark the kitchen had suddenly become.

'I think we're in for a storm,' said Dad. 'I'll put some more lights on.' He got up from the table and Bob Redmay said,

'If it's going to be as bad as it looks, maybe we should

think about going. It's not a long drive, but in this weather—'

He didn't get any further before a blue flash lit up the room, followed two seconds later by the enormous bang and roll of a thunderclap. Chelsea screamed, and as the echoes rumbled away Katy wailed with fear from upstairs.

'Oh dear, I'd better see to her,' said Mrs McCarthy. She hurried out, and they could hear her calling as she ran up the stairs, 'It's all right, Kitten-Kat; Mummy's coming, there's nothing to be frightened of . . .'

Another flash blasted through the house; the thunder took longer to come this time but it was still deafening. Chelsea pushed her plate away and went to sit next to her mother, and Bob said, 'Hell, we should have seen this coming. Look, if everyone gets their coats, maybe we can make it to the car before the rain starts.'

'No, Dad!' Chelsea protested. 'I don't want to go outside!'

'It's OK, hon, we won't get hit,' he reassured. 'Safer in a car than a house. I'm real sorry, Chris,' to Mr McCarthy, 'but I really think we'd better go. Give our apologies to Alison, will you?'

As he said it, the rain began. The noise was astonishing; in the space of a second it was hammering on the roof and walls and windows as if hundreds of demented drummers were out there giving it everything they'd got. The next flash was so bright that everyone flinched, and the thunder that accompanied it was almost simultaneous.

'Oops,' said Mr McCarthy. 'I'd better unplug the phone and the TV aerial – that one was a bit too close for comfort!'

He headed for the sitting-room. Dublin had started to bark; he was more annoyed than frightened, and seemed to think that the more he barked, the more likely the storm would be to go away. In the noisy confusion the Redmays got ready to leave. Chelsea was still frightened and protesting, but amid more flashes and bangs she was helped into her jacket and, with hasty farewells and apologies, the family made a run for their hired car. Mrs McCarthy came down with Katy in time to hear the engine start up, and she peered out of the window as they drove away.

'I hope they get back safely,' she said. 'Just look at that *rain*!'

'We'll be borrowing Holly's boat at this rate,' said Tom's dad. He had taken Katy on his lap and was jogging her up and down to distract her from the storm.

'Oh, Holly!' Mrs McCarthy turned round. 'You can't possibly *think* of going home the way you came! We'll drive you back; though maybe we ought to wait until the worst's over, so if you want to phone your parents—'

There was a searing sound overhead and a blinding flash blotted everything out. Tom's brain hardly had time to register it before a gargantuan crash shook the house from end to end, and all the lights went out. Dublin howled and jumped halfway across the kitchen, Katy shrieked, and Mrs McCarthy leaped back from the window with a yell of shock. Tom yelled too, but he couldn't even hear himself, the din was so huge. It turned into a rolling, bawling roar, and they all froze, white-faced with shock, as they listened to it.

'Thunderbolt!' said Dad shakily, when it was finally possible to hear anything else at all. 'My God, that was a near one!'

'W-we're not hit, are we?' Mum quavered.

'No – if we were, we'd know it by now. Here, look after Kitten-Kat, will you? I'll light some candles.'

He handed over the sobbing Katy and groped in the dimness to the kitchen drawer. Tom's eyesight had recovered enough for him to make out vague shapes in the gloom, but he was relieved when the candles were found and lit.

'What a racket!' said his father. 'It's probably taken out the whole village's electricity supply.'

'I hope that's the worst it's done,' Mum said shakily.

'Well, I'm not going outside to look now! We'll find out in the morning. Come on; I don't suppose anyone feels like eating any more, so let's get the table cleared. Holly, I think you should ring your parents. They might be getting worried.'

Holly said, 'OK, thanks, Mr McCarthy,' and went to the phone in the hall. But she was soon back.

'The phone line's dead,' she said. 'The thunderbolt

must have taken it out. I tried my mobile, but I can't get a signal on that, either.'

'Chris, I think we should take her home, before it gets any worse,' said Tom's mum.

Mr McCarthy agreed. He was fetching his waterproof and boots when, above the racket of the rain, they heard another noise.

'It sounds like a car,' said Mum. She looked outside. 'It's the Redmays! They're back!'

She opened the door as the hire car stopped and the Redmays came running to the house.

'I'm sorry, Alison,' said Bob Redmay breathlessly, 'but we couldn't get through! There's a tree down – hit by that bolt, by the looks of it – and the road's flooding up by the bridge. We had water up to the axles and the engine nearly died on us. We had to come back.'

'Come in, quickly, all of you!' Mrs McCarthy shut the door as a surge of rain tried to follow them. Another flash, though more distant, lit up the kitchen, and in the light of it Tom saw that Chelsea had been crying. He suddenly felt sorry for her.

'We hate to impose,' Jane Redmay began, 'but—'

'Don't be silly; of course you're not imposing! We're just thankful the tree didn't fall on you! Now look, everyone's going to stay the night – you too, Holly; even if the emergency services can get to the road blockage in this, it'll be hours before it's cleared. We haven't got many spare rooms, but there are plenty of blankets and duvets, so we'll manage.' She glanced at her husband, who had come back. 'Chris, if you take Kitten-Kat again, I'll go and sort things out. Tom and Holly can help me.'

The storm gradually died away, rumbling off into the north-east until all that remained was an occasional distant flicker and rumble. But the rain didn't let up. Tom could hear it rushing and gurgling in the gutters as he and Holly helped Mrs McCarthy arrange sleeping places for everyone. Bob and Jane were given the spare room, the two Redmay boys shared with Tom, and Holly and Chelsea were to have Katy's room while Katy went in with her parents. An assortment of mattresses, sofa cushions and anything else that would do for makeshift beds was found, and by the time real darkness fell, as opposed to the unnatural dark of the storm, all was ready.

Even Jack didn't protest at the idea of going to bed early, and well before midnight almost everyone was asleep.

Only Tom was having problems. Thoughts were going round and round in his head and his mind refused to calm down. Maybe it was sharing his room with Robbie and Jack that made him restless, he wondered. It was dark, and he couldn't actually see the two boys on their cushion beds, but he knew they were there, and he wasn't used to it. Or maybe he was still worrying about the fact that nothing unpleasant had happened – yet.

He did drift off eventually, and began to dream. In the

dream someone was talking to him. He didn't know who it was, but they kept saying 'No' to something. Then suddenly, clear as a bell, they said: '*Danger!*'

Tom started awake, and was just in time to see Susannah come in through the solid barrier of the bedroom door.

'*Ah!*' Tom slapped a hand to his mouth in shock. A weird, chilly light flickered around Susannah as she hovered at the end of his bed. She wasn't looking at him but at a point beyond him; and she seemed to be shouting something but he couldn't hear her. Then, in his head, the sound came.

'No, no, no! No, you cannot, you must not – *danger!*'

'Susannah, what is it?' Forgetting Robbie and Jack, Tom started to scramble out of bed and go to her. But Susannah receded, gliding backwards to the door.

'*No!*' she cried one more time. Then she was gone, and the light with her, leaving him in total darkness.

Tom stood gaping idiotically as all sorts of awful possibilities tumbled through his mind. What had Susannah meant? Who was in danger? Or had the whole thing been a dream?

He flung a glance in Robbie and Jack's direction, but there was no sound. They hadn't woken . . . As quickly as he could without making a noise, Tom groped his way out of the bedroom – and ran slap into Holly on the landing.

They looked at each other in the light of Holly's

finger-shaded torch, and said together, 'Susannah's been—'

Both stopped. 'You saw her, too?' Holly whispered.

He nodded, telling her what had happened.

'She did exactly the same to me!' Holly hissed. 'Something's wrong, Tom, it's got to be! Did Jack and Robbie wake up?'

'No, luckily. Chelsea?'

'She's asleep, too.'

'I'd better get dressed, and then we'll go and investigate.'

'OK.' Holly had slept in her clothes, but Tom didn't want to risk going back to his room. 'There's some stuff for the wash in the laundry basket,' he said. 'Go downstairs and I'll see you in a minute.'

Holly hurried away, and Tom ran to the bathroom, where he raided the basket and dressed in ten seconds flat. He heard Dublin yelp a delighted welcome in the kitchen, but luckily Holly managed to stop him from making any more noise.

'Get your torch; we might need two,' said Holly. 'Can I borrow your mum's wellies? I left my shoes upstairs.'

'Yeah; in the porch. Bring mine, too.'

Holly came back with the boots and said, 'There's a weird noise outside.'

'Uh? What sort of noise? I can't hear anything.'

'You can't, from here. But it sounds like water rushing.'

'The gutters, I expect,' said Tom, hauling his boots on. 'They're probably all overflowing by now.'

'It's too loud to be gutters. Hang on a minute . . .' Holly went out again. Then:

'Tom, *quick*! Come and look!'

She was in the piano-room. The window looked out on the steep bank behind the mill, and when Tom rushed in she had opened the curtains and was staring in horror.

It was still raining, and the bank was just a black wall, even darker than the sky. But the shine of water was unmistakable. It was falling over the bank's edge, streaming down in rivulets from the top.

'The millpond's overflowed!' said Holly.

Tom was stunned. 'It can't have done! There's an outlet; it should all be going back to the stream!'

'Well, it isn't. Something must have blocked it. Tom, we'd better —' She stopped, tensing.

'What?' he said.

'Up there . . .' Holly's voice was a taut whisper. 'On the top of the bank. I saw a light.'

Tom peered, and was about to say, 'You imagined it,' when he saw it, too. A quick flicker in the darkness, like a torch beam. Then it showed again. It *was* a torch, and behind it was a human shape. A small shape . . .

The same thought hit them both together.

'*Jack*!'

13

'It can't be him!' Tom said, horrified. 'He's asleep upstairs!'

'Is he?' Holly countered grimly. 'I mean, did you actually *see* him?'

'No.' Tom swallowed. 'It was too dark . . .' Susannah's warning rang in his memory. 'Oh, God; if he's been lured out there . . .'

'Come on!' Holly urged. 'We've got to get to him, fast!'

They ran out through the back door into the rain. Dublin followed, but there was no time to shut him in; they just had to hope that he wouldn't start barking and wake everyone else.

The bobbing torch had vanished, but they had a rough idea of where Jack must be, and hurried to the bank. More water was coming down it with every minute, and Tom said, 'We're going to have to find what's blocking it, or we'll have a full-scale flood on our hands!'

'Never mind that now. Let's find Jack!'

But when they tried to tackle the bank, they quickly realized that it was impossible. The whole slope had become a perilous mudslide; their feet simply couldn't get a grip, and even Dublin scrabbled to no avail.

'Have to go round the long way, by the track,' Holly said, panting with effort.

Suddenly Dublin gave his yelp-bark. They turned, torches swinging round –

And the beams lit up Chelsea standing right behind them.

'What's going on?' Chelsea was bareheaded and in light shoes, though she had slung someone else's coat hastily over her shoulders.

Tom was about to say, 'Nothing,' but realized that that would be pretty dumb. 'It's the millpond,' he said. 'It's overflowing.'

'Well, you'd better wake your mom and dad, then, hadn't you?' She turned for the house, and desperately Holly said, 'No! Wait a minute –'

Chelsea stopped and stared challengingly. 'Yeah?'

'We don't want to wake them up,' said Holly. 'You see . . . it isn't just the pond.' She looked at Tom, and he nodded.

'We'd better tell her. She's guessed half of it, anyway.'

'I sure have,' Chelsea's glare turned to a triumphant smile. 'There's a ghost, isn't there? A ghost called Susannah. That's why you're out here. You're ghost-hunting!' She put her fists on her hips. 'Well, I'm coming too!'

'Chelsea,' said Holly, 'it isn't as simple as that. OK, yes, there is a ghost called Susannah. But there's something else, too. Something dangerous. It—'

She broke off in mid-sentence as Dublin started to growl.

They all turned quickly to look at the dog. Dublin's hackles were up and his head was lowered menacingly, teeth showing in the torchlight. He was staring towards the millrace.

'What is it?' Chelsea said sharply. 'What's he seen?'

Tom's heart bumped hard and fast, and the hairs on the back of his neck began to prickle.

'Shine your torch!' urged Chelsea. 'There's something there!'

'No,' Tom said harshly. 'I know what's there. And I don't want to see it.'

Dublin growled again, and the growl became a snarl. He started to back away – then he turned and bolted for the house with his tail between his legs.

Chelsea's face turned white. 'What's bugging him?' she demanded shrilly. '*Just tell me what's going on!*'

There was only one thing Tom could do. He took a deep breath and said, 'Chelsea, listen to me. There isn't time to explain everything, but we think your little brother's in danger, and—'

'Jack, in danger?' Chelsea's voice shot up the scale.

'Yes! Stop interrupting, will you! Jack's out here somewhere – Holly and I saw him – and we think he's been lured by the—'

'The thing that's haunting the mill,' Holly cut in hastily, before Tom could say the word 'demon'. 'So the most important thing is to find him before he gets hurt!'

'Well, why didn't you say? Where is he? We've got to go get him!'

Tom was fazed. He had expected her to argue, or at the very least waste time with awkward questions. Instead, she just accepted what she had been told, and wanted to do something about it.

'We can sort it,' he said. 'You go back indoors.'

'The heck with that! It's my kid brother we're talking about – let's *go*!'

Tom and Holly looked at each other and shrugged. 'OK,' said Holly. 'This way!'

Getting up the track wasn't much easier than trying to climb the bank. Water was pouring down in a mini-river, and for every three steps of ground they made they seemed to slither two steps back. But they made it at last, and as their heads came level with the bank top they saw that the millpond had become a shining, sinister lake spreading far beyond its normal boundaries.

'Wow!' Holly breathed. 'It's going to be right over the top soon!'

Tom was suddenly torn between the urgency of finding Jack and the other, perhaps greater urgency of stopping the rise of the water. He hesitated, not knowing what to do – then suddenly Holly cried, 'There he is!'

A torch beam was bobbing and jumping on the far side of the pond, by the outlet that should have been taking the water back to the stream. They started to run towards it, Tom calling a warning to be careful on the slippery edge. Chelsea shouted Jack's name as they approached, and with huge relief Tom heard the distant reply.

'Guys! C'mon and give me some help here!'

Their torches lit a small figure at the pondside. Jack was almost unrecognizable under a coating of mud, but he was grinning broadly. One hand held his torch, and in the other was a spar of wood.

'Hey, cool!' he greeted them. 'You showed up right on time!' He pointed at the overflow. 'I've been trying to clear this, but I could do with some help.'

The outlet, Tom saw, was blocked. There were several stones that hadn't been there before, clods of earth and grass, a tangle of sticks . . . It wasn't a natural blockage. Someone had deliberately tried to make a dam, and mud and twigs washed down by the flood had turned it into a solid barrier.

He glared at Jack. 'Who put those stones and stuff there?'

'We-ell . . .' Jack didn't meet his glare. 'I only wanted to see what would happen. You know?'

'Yeah, I know, all right!' Now Tom realized what the small boy had been doing up here on his own this afternoon. 'You might have flooded the whole house and mill and everything, you idiot!'

'I'm sorry!' Then Jack brightened. 'But I did come try and clear it, didn't I?'

Tom said something under his breath, snatched the wooden spar from him and shoved one end, hard, into the tangle of the blockage. At once he knew that it wasn't going to give easily; the whole thing felt solid as rock. Holly added her weight and they put all their strength into it. But the spar only bent and groaned and threatened to snap, and the solid mass didn't shift.

'We'd better – get – Dad and Mr Redmay!' Tom panted. 'We can't do this on our own!'

'Aw, no!' Jack pleaded. 'I'll get it if Dad and Mom find out!'

'You'll get it a lot worse if the whole pond overflows!' Tom growled. 'Holly, can you go and wake the others?'

'I'll do it,' said Chelsea quickly. 'It's my dumb brother's fault, after all, and Holly's bigger; she'll be more use here.'

'OK. Tell them to bring crowbars, or something. Here's a torch.' Tom gave her his, watched until she had safely negotiated the pond's edge and reached the track, then bent to his task again. He was livid with Jack; but underneath the anger was also an overwhelming feeling of relief. He knew, now, why Susannah had come to warn him and Holly of danger. But they had reacted in time; no one was hurt, and the house wouldn't be flooded. If they could just shift one section of the blockage, the pressure of water would do the rest . . .

He and Holly leaned on the spar again. For several minutes they pushed and pulled and wrestled, while Jack yelled encouragement. But it was useless.

'Chelsea must have woken everyone by now,' Holly said as they took a much-needed breather.

Tom glanced towards the house, but from where they were standing the bank blocked the view of everything but the roof. 'It'll take them a couple of minutes to get dressed and get the crowbars,' he pointed out. 'Come on – we'd better have another go.'

They started to push and pull again. Suddenly Jack called, 'Uh-oh! Watch out, it's—' but before he could say the word 'breaking' there was a groan and a splintering noise, and the wooden spar split in half.

Tom stumbled backwards, nearly lost his balance, and flailed his arms to steady himself. 'Oh, *brilliant*!' He peered at the outlet, where half of the spar now stuck up like a crazy ship's mast.

Holly gulped a deep breath. 'Never mind,' she said. 'We weren't getting anywhere, anyway. Just have to wait for the others.'

Jack piped up, 'Hey, how about if—' But Tom was in the wrong mood.

'Whatever it is, I don't want to know!' he interrupted grouchily. 'You've caused enough trouble already, so just shut up.'

'But if we—'

'I said, shut *up*. One more word and I'll be tempted to chuck you in the pond.'

'Leave it, Tom,' Holly said. 'There's no point going for him.' She gave Jack a warning look of her own. 'I'll go and see if they're coming. They should be, by now.'

She picked her way carefully to the bank's edge and looked over. She expected to see the flicker of candlelight in windows, but to her surprise and dismay, the house was still in darkness. There was no light anywhere at all.

Except . . .

'Tom,' she said in an odd, tight voice, 'come here. Quickly.'

Tom squelched across to join her, Jack at his heels.

'What do you make of that?' asked Holly.

He looked. The rain and the darkness had blurred everything into a featureless dark grey. But down by the millrace there was a single gleam of light. It looked as though it was at ground level, but it was hard to be sure. It lit up nothing more interesting than a patch of wet grass.

'What is it?' said Holly.

Jack pushed between them and peered, too. 'It's a torch, of course,' he said airily. 'Chelsea's, I bet. She must have dropped it. And she calls *me* dumb!'

No lights in the house. No sound of anyone coming to help. Chelsea's torch dropped and abandoned on the ground . . . the stark truth crept up on Tom and Holly like cold, rising water.

Holly whispered, 'Oh, no . . . it can't have . . .'

Oh, it can, replied a small, terrible voice in Tom's head. *It must have been waiting for her. And all this time it was Jack we thought it wanted, because he's the youngest. But it didn't*

want him at all. It wanted a girl. Another girl; just like
Susannah . . .

The frozen helplessness that had gripped him suddenly
let go its hold.

'Come on!' he yelled. '*Move!*'

He didn't stop to think about the dangerous descent
but went straight over the edge of the bank and started
to slide and slither down. Holly went after him, leaving
Jack at the top shouting, 'Hey, guys! What about me?
Where's the fire?' They ignored him; for a few moments
he thought of following them down the bank, but he
didn't have the nerve. Turning, he pelted towards the
track.

Tom's feet went from under him when he was halfway
down, and he careered to the bottom in a mini tidal
wave of water and liquid mud. Holly crashed into him as
he was staggering to his feet, and together they ran
towards the millrace.

Chelsea's torch lay where it had fallen. Tom snatched
it up and he and Holly pointed the two beams at the
millwheel.

The wheel sprang to view in stark angles of light and
shadow. But there was nothing else there. With a sick
feeling Tom shone his torch down into the channel of
the race, half expecting to see Chelsea lying unconscious
and badly injured on the rough stones. Relief hit him as
he saw the channel was empty.

'Scan along the ledge!' Holly hissed.

Jack was shouting and waving his own torch as he scrabbled his way down the track, but neither of them even heard. Their twin lights' beams tracked quickly along the stone ledge on the far side of the millrace; for a second or two they thought it was deserted, but then –

'*There it is!*' Quick movement in the circle cast by Holly's torch, and a flapping shape went scuttling along the ledge and out of the light's reach.

'It's heading towards the bridge!' Tom said.

'Chelsea can't be there; she'd never manage the climb up to it with all that mud!' Nonetheless Holly swung her torch to the bridge.

Chelsea was there.

She was standing at the edge of the bridge, holding tightly to the first of the posts that supported the decayed wooden rail. Her body was rigid, her eyes stared straight ahead, and even from this distance they could see she was in a complete trance.

An appalling giggle sounded from the far side of the bridge and the water-demon's hunched form appeared on the fringe of the torchlight. Its long, stick-thin arms worked in a jerky, beckoning motion . . . and Chelsea stretched out one foot towards the bridge.

'Chelsea, don't!' But even as he shouted, Tom knew it was useless. Chelsea couldn't hear him. She was hypnotized, caught like a fly in a spider's web; all she knew was that she *had* to go, *had* to answer the deadly summons.

'*Chelsea!*' Tom yelled again. And even as his voice rang out, another, higher pitched scream echoed it.

'*You leave my sister alone!*'

Jack raced past them so fast that they didn't have a chance of stopping him. He hurled himself at the bank, hands reaching and clawing, determined to get to the top no matter what—

'NO!'

Jack yelled in shock and reeled backwards as Susannah materialized right in front of him. A weird aura danced around her, turning her figure to a ghastly blue-green; for the first time she looked *terrifying*.

'Leave her!' Susannah commanded. 'It is too late for her now! Let her go!'

Chelsea had taken her first step on to the bridge, oblivious to everything but the lurking, beckoning demon. Horrified, Tom realized what Susannah was doing. If the demon took Chelsea, she would be freed. With himself and Holly she had resisted the terrible temptation; but Chelsea was another matter. Chelsea was not her friend. Chelsea had not tried to help her. And Chelsea was descended from the family who had abandoned her to her fate two hundred years ago.

Jack had backed away from Susannah; he collided with Tom and clutched him, shivering. On the bridge Chelsea had taken another two steps, and suddenly Tom's stalled brain snapped free. There was only one hope.

'Susannah!' he called out. 'You can't let her die! She

hasn't harmed you; what happened to you wasn't her fault! We've got to save her – help us, *please*!'

'No!' Susannah's head turned and she glared at him. 'This is *my* chance!'

'Surely there's another way?' Holly pleaded.

'. . . No.' But did Susannah hesitate before she said it? Holly snatched at the possibility.

'There must be!'

'It wouldn't work! You are not strong enough!'

So there *was* something! 'Susannah, you can't get your freedom like this!' As a vicar's daughter, Holly grabbed at the one thing that might shake Susannah's determination. 'What about your *soul*?'

Susannah's aura flickered wildly. She had been brought up in an age when people believed firmly in heaven and hell, and Holly's warning shook her to the core.

'No . . .' she quavered. 'There will be forgiveness!'

'Want to bet?' Tom shouted. 'What if there isn't?'

'Susannah, we want to help you *and* save Chelsea!' cried Holly. 'If there's a way, tell us, now!'

Jack looked fearfully up at Tom. 'She's got to tell!' he said piteously. 'I know Chelsea can be a pain in the butt, but – she's my *sister*!'

Susannah looked quickly at the small boy. Her mouth worked and distorted as if she was about to cry, and the weird aura flickered and danced again. Then, so fast that they all jumped, she whirled round and flew – literally *flew*, Tom realized much later – away from them, towards the bridge. Chelsea was halfway across, moving in a peculiar, shuffling way, as if someone was remote-controlling her limbs. Reaching the bridge, Susannah pointed to her and called out piercingly:

'Cousin! Stop!'

Chelsea jolted as if she had had an electric shock, and on the ledge the demon uttered a shrill, whistling cry of fury. Susannah's aura dipped and flared again. 'I don't fear your threats!' she called back defiantly. 'What more can you do to me?' She reached towards Chelsea. 'Wake, cousin! *Wake!*'

Chelsea woke. Tom and Holly couldn't imagine what she felt when she saw where she was and what confronted her, but the scream she let out went through to their bones. Then she burst into tears.

'Chelsea!' Jack yelled. He twisted out of Tom's grasp and ran to the bank. 'Chelsea, come back here, *quick!*'

The bridge creaked ominously and Chelsea screamed again. 'I c-c-can't . . .' she wailed. 'I'm so scared . . .'

Jack was trying and failing to scramble up the bank. Tom and Holly ran to him, Tom shouting to Susannah.

'Help her! Get her back!'

'I cannot touch her!' Susannah cried. 'I can only add my will to hers, but that won't be enough! There is only one way to defeat it!'

'*How?*'

'By sending it away from the lair it has made! Water can drive it out – but it won't go willingly; it is too full of hate!' The demon uttered another enraged cry and Susannah flinched. 'Tom, it's no use! You are not strong enough! You are not, you are *not*!'

Water . . . Tom flung a wild glance up the bank. The pond was overflowing more drastically now, the thin streams starting to merge together. Soon, the water would be cascading down in a single sheet. But it wouldn't have sufficient power . . .

'Tom, couldn't we dig a ditch?' Jack begged desperately. 'Send the water down the mill thing?'

'What? No, don't be crazy; that's −' Then understanding slammed into Tom's consciousness. The sheer weight of water in the millpond must be enormous. And up there, unused since Susannah's time, was the outlet gate. Not the one Jack had tempered with, but the sluice-gate, that used to send water down the race to drive the millwheel . . .

He grabbed Holly's arm ferociously. 'The race!' he shouted. 'If we could open the old gate −'

Her eyes widened. '*Yes*! But the water'll be like a tidal wave − we've got to get Chelsea off the bridge before it comes through!'

Tom's nerves took a huge lurch but he pushed them away. 'I'll do it,' he said. 'You get a crowbar; go up and—'

'No!' Holly interrupted. 'You're stronger than me. And you know where everything is; I'd waste time. Susannah'll help me. *I'll* get Chelsea!'

Tom hesitated. He wanted to say a hundred things,

like, 'You can't', and 'It's too dangerous' and 'I won't let you'. But that wouldn't cut any ice with Holly...

A hand tugged at his sleeve and Jack begged, 'Guys, stop arguing! Just *do* something!'

'Tom, *go*!' Holly said. And before Tom could respond, she was heading for the bank.

Tom paused for two seconds more. Then, with Jack at his heels, he raced away towards the door of the mill.

14

How she had done it Tom couldn't begin to imagine, but when he and Jack came out of the mill with iron crowbars in their hands, Holly was almost at the top of the bank. It was a weird, nightmarish scene. Chelsea still stood frozen in the middle of the bridge, her figure lit by the greenish glow that surrounded Susannah; now, though, Susannah had got past her – *or through her*? Tom wondered, then pushed the thought hurriedly away – and was standing like a protecting angel between her and the thing on the ledge.

Holly reached the top and stood up, panting for breath. Torchlight danced on the bridge and Tom heard her call out.

'Chelsea, it's Holly! I'm here – can you come towards me?'

'N . . . nooo . . .' Chelsea's voice quavered back. 'I'm scaaared . . .'

A shadow shifted and swirled in the blackness beyond the bridge. The monstrosity was there. It knew that Susannah was blocking the way to its victim. But it also knew that time was on its side. Chelsea's stamina couldn't last for much longer. Her will would break soon; and when it did, Susannah would be powerless to stop her doing exactly what the demon wanted her to do.

Jack said, 'Tom, let's *go!*' and Tom snapped back to earth. They took off towards the track. Jack's crowbar was almost too heavy for him and he dragged it, staggering; Tom didn't wait but rushed on ahead. He had hoped against hope that someone would come running out of the house. But the bulk of the mill building blocked sound. No one had woken, no one had heard them, and there wasn't enough time left to go and raise the alarm.

He tackled the track at a full charge, pounding to the top and using the iron bar like a ski pole to help him. Jack was shouting at him to wait, but he couldn't afford to. As he ran round the pond, horribly aware that he might slip and plunge in, he could see Holly below him. She was on the bridge now, moving slowly and cautiously towards the paralyzed Chelsea. And the bridge was starting to sag . . .

'Holly, be careful!' Tom yelled. He jumped the outlet where Jack's meddling had dammed it, miraculously landed upright on the other side, and pelted to where his joggling torchlight showed the old sluice-gate. The gate had been securely blocked off, but Dad's excavations had shifted some of the stone; safe enough at the time, for the overflow had kept the pond level low enough for the sluice to be dry. Now though, Tom could see the sheen of water pressing and pushing against the dam. It wouldn't take too much to breach it. It *mustn't* take too much . . .

Not really knowing what he was doing but acting on a desperate instinct, Tom reached the sluice, dropped his torch and rammed one end of the crowbar straight down into the dam. The bar jumped and recoiled as it hit stone, and a jarring pain went through his hands.

'Tom, wait for me!' Jack was coming, looking like a small demon himself in the dark. Tom helped him scramble the last couple of metres, and Jack tried to push his own bar into the dam.

'Not like that! Here, give it to me!' Tom rammed his own bar again; it went home this time and he grabbed the other bar from Jack.

'That's it!' Both bars were in place. 'Now, lean on it! Lean as hard as you can!'

They threw their weight on the bars, straining and grunting with effort. Nothing happened, nothing gave; Tom wanted to scream with frustration but didn't have the breath —

Then suddenly the bar in his hands shifted fractionally.

'It's moving!' His voice cracked with excitement. 'Push, Jack! *Push!*'

Jack let out a sort of yodelling yell and his feet almost lifted off the ground as he gave it everything he could. The water was pushing, too; a huge, solid pressure weakening the wall of stone and wood and earth . . .

'*It's going!*' Jack shrieked triumphantly.

There was a splintering groan, then a grating sound, as the gate bulged away from the pond. Water spurted through a crack; a trickle at first, but the crack was widening –

Tom thrust the bar away from him and stumbled to the edge of the bank. Below, Holly had reached Chelsea. She had an arm around her and was trying to coax her back. But Chelsea was resisting; Tom could hear her wails of terror.

'Holly!' Tom bawled. 'Holly, the gate's going! *Get off the bridge!*'

And then the dam gave way.

Tom heard the splashing roar as the massed weight of water came powering through the breach. The whole world seemed to slow down: like a movie rolling in slow motion before him he saw Holly struggling to drag Chelsea back from the swaying bridge, Susannah with her hands to her face, crying out wordlessly. Chelsea was screaming too, but her voice was lost behind the rising noise of water thundering down the first section of the channel and into the race.

The leading wave hit the bottom, hurling spray in all directions, and in seconds the old, dry channel of the millrace became a churning cataract. The millwheel jumped and juddered as the water hit it; the great frame was rusted solid and it couldn't turn, so it took the full force of the water's power. It wouldn't stand the onslaught for long – it would be smashed to pieces, and when it went, the bridge would surely go too –

'*Holly!*' Tom flung himself down the bank, not thinking

of the risk, only frantic to reach Holly and Chelsea before the bridge shook itself apart under them. The slope pitched him forward and he fell, rolling, tumbling, churning to the bottom twice as fast as he had gone before. Bruised and half stunned he staggered to his feet, started towards the bridge –

With a splintering and cracking audible even over the thunder of water, the millwheel began to break up. Spars of wood went spinning and whirling away, some hitting the bridge and shaking it from end to end. Then suddenly the wheel was wrenched loose. It slewed; the ancient fixings broke free, sending chunks of stone and mortar plummeting into the race. The whole structure began to fall – and on the ledge beyond the race there was a rush of movement.

'*Look out!*' But Tom had no time for the words to come out before the demon came hurtling across the shuddering bridge. Clawed hands reached, trying to grasp at Holly and Chelsea – but Susannah shrieked a furious challenge and whirled to face the oncoming horror. They met, collided, and in a stunning moment the two of them merged into a single flailing, fighting shape.

'Holly, move, MOVE!' But Holly was already moving. Desperation gave her new strength and she was dragging Chelsea with her, clinging to the rail with her free hand, struggling for the bank.

She made solid ground with three seconds to spare. Tom was there, Jack somehow beside him; they grabbed hands, arms, clothing, hauling the girls to safety. Holly and Chelsea collapsed, gasping; Jack fell with them in a tangle of arms and legs – so only Tom saw the bridge begin its final collapse.

The rail went first, snapping and splitting and falling sideways into the water below. Then the planks of the walkway came apart – and with a human scream and a whistling, unhuman howl, the flickering, battling chaos that was Susannah and the demon plunged down into the race and were swept away under the shattered wheel.

Horrified, Tom yelled Susannah's name, but there was no answering cry, and all he could see was the water crashing and pounding over the wheel's remains. Without thinking, without pausing, he began to run, following the millrace channel as it coursed on its way back to the natural stream. Rationally he knew he couldn't help Susannah, but he had to try! He didn't see the new torch beams stabbing the darkness, didn't hear the voices that shouted from the house as the adults woke up at last and came rushing out. Reaching the far end of the garden, Tom plunged in among the trees. At once the path turned sharply downwards; branches whipped his face and he grabbed at saplings to help him stay on his feet. He could hear the stream, though he couldn't see it; the noise was incredible as the mass of water from the millrace swelled it to a roaring torrent. On Tom stumbled, on and down. He wanted to call out to Susannah, but he didn't have the breath, and she couldn't have heard him. He *had* to try to find her!

He burst out on to the foreshore so suddenly that it was all he could do not to carry on running straight into the creek. Slithering to a halt in the loose shingle, he yelled into the dark.

'Susannah! *Susannah!*'

He could hear the flooded stream tumbling explosively into the creek a little way off, but that was all. The sky held a hint of paler grey behind the low, ragged clouds; moonlight or dawn, Tom didn't know, but it was enough to show the creek water sliding rapidly seawards. The tide was going out, and running fast . . . He had a sudden crazy impulse to jump into Holly's moored boat, start the engine and try to chase the outflowing stream. But common sense came to his rescue in time, and instead he ran, jumping rocks and patches of seaweed, to where the stream erupted out of the wood and into the creek.

As he reached it, an eerie howl echoed out of the darkness.

Tom stopped and his whole body tingled with gooseflesh. *What was that sound?* He had seemed to hear it with his spine, and he stood motionless, holding his breath. The sound came again, closer this time, like the wailing whistle of an old-fashioned train, approaching at tremendous speed. Then he saw what was hurtling towards him down the stream, tumbling over and over in a helpless white-water ride. Jerking arms, clawing hands, a twisted body covered in tattered weed that roiled and tangled in the current – Tom stumbled back as the demon went thrashing past. For one heart-stopping moment he saw its face; the phosphorescent skin, the dead-fish eyes, the mouth gaping like a hole in decaying jelly as it screamed its rage and despair. Then with a swirl and welter of bubbles it was carried into the creek, and the powerful river current swept it away downstream. One final cry and it was gone, leaving Tom standing on the shore, staring at the place where it had vanished.

He was still there, wanting to move but unable to make any part of his body do what it was supposed to, when light stabbed jerkily from the wood and someone came crashing through the trees on to the shingle.

'Tom!' Holly's voice shook with relief, exhaustion and fright all at once. 'Are you all right?'

Tom nodded. He couldn't speak as Holly slid to a stop and took hold of his arm.

'What happened? The demon, Susannah – where did they go?'

He waved at the creek, swallowed hard and finally found his voice. 'It – it went into the river. Carried away on the tide. But Susannah . . . I don't know.'

Behind them, Susannah said, 'I'm here, Tom.'

They spun round. Susannah was standing three metres away. The ragged green aura was gone; instead just a faint, pale light glowed around her, barely enough for them to make out her face. She looked very calm.

'Susannah . . .' Holly whispered. 'Is it . . . gone?'

Susannah nodded. 'Truly gone. The river has it now, and soon the river will give it to the sea. It will not find the strength to come back.'

'And – and you . . .' Holly gulped, hardly daring to ask the question. 'Can you go now, too? Are you free?'

The ghost looked around, at the wood, the creek, the torrential rush of the stream, and smiled. 'Yes,' she said.

There was so much Tom wanted to say to Susannah, but he couldn't find the right words; couldn't find any words at all. Susannah seemed to understand. She gazed at him and her smile became something very private.

'I, too, have no words,' she said. 'For either of you. Except to say that the debt I owe you is the greatest there could be. Thank you, dear Tom and Holly.' She moved one foot on the shingle. It made no sound. 'I shall go now. Goodbye, my dearest and truest friends. If such a thing is possible for me, I will never forget you.'

And a moment later, she was no longer there.

Tom suddenly felt as if his legs had turned to porridge, and before Holly could do anything to steady him he sat down with a heavy thump. Neither of them said anything for perhaps a minute. Then Holly spoke.

'Everyone in the house woke up. Nobody's noticed you're missing yet and they didn't see me sneak away. Oh, and your parents think the millpond broke its banks by itself.'

It was as if she needed to say something banal to keep

201

herself on an even keel, and Tom gratefully joined in.

'What about Chelsea?' he asked.

'She's OK. Badly shocked, but I think that's all. Your mum and Mrs Redmay took her to the house.' Holly paused. 'I don't know how much she'll remember, or how much of it she'll believe. But I don't think she'll ever tell anyone what really happened.'

'Jack might,' said Tom.

'Oh, sure. But he's a kid. Everyone'll think he's making it all up.' Holly giggled, a little bit hysterically. 'He thinks the whole thing was really cool.'

Tom was trying to think of a comment to make to that, just for the sake of answering, when they both heard a familiar barking coming from the wood.

'I don't believe it!' Tom peered into the dark. 'How on earth did he know where we'd gone? Dublin! Here, Dublin!'

'You'd better get on your feet before he arrives and jumps all over you.' Holly grabbed his arm and hauled him upright. Moments later Dublin came hurtling out of the wood and hurled himself joyfully at them, yelping and panting and pawing and wagging.

'All right, all right! Get down, you idiot dog!' Tom was laughing, though part of him felt like crying, too, and he didn't know why. 'How did you find us, huh? You can't possibly have followed our scent in all this rain!'

'He's telepathic, that's what,' said Holly, dragging Dublin away from his efforts to knock Tom down and sit on him. Then she looked speculatively at the path. 'We'd better go. It's going to be a godawful slog up there, and if we don't get back soon someone'll miss us.'

'They'll think we've been washed away.'

'Yeah. They wouldn't be far wrong, either. Would they?'

They exchanged a look that, for the first time, expressed everything without the need for words. Then Tom laughed explosively.

'What's so funny?' Holly demanded.

The laugh turned into a snort and Tom wiped his nose on his sleeve. 'I just thought . . . I bet you wish you'd stayed sulking and never made friends with me!'

'What, and miss all this? Not a chance! Anyway, without me you'd have made a complete hash of the whole thing, so it's just as well I did decide to speak to you after all!'

Tom pulled a face at her. 'OK, then. Seeing as you're such a genius, *you* can think up a story to explain it all to Mum and Dad!'

Holly laughed, too, then sobered. 'I don't think it'll be too difficult,' she said. 'After all, even the unlikeliest story's going to be easier for them to believe than the truth. Whatever else happens, that's going to stay *our* secret.'

Tom nodded, knowing she was right. But did it matter? Susannah was at rest, and the danger was gone. The haunting of Trevenna Mill was truly over.

He looked at the creek, at the tide that had carried

the demon away. It wouldn't return. It never could. It *never* could. Could it?

The thought faded and he turned to Holly again. 'Come on. Let's get back, before the search and rescue helicopters arrive.'

'In your dreams!' said Holly with another laugh.

With Dublin bounding ahead of them they started up the path, leaving the shore to the night. The sounds of their feet and voices faded, and soon there was only the noise of the flooding stream as it continued its chaotic rush to the creek, and on to the river and the sea.